The Daring Young Man on the Flying Trapeze

AND OTHER STORIES

Also Available by William Saroyan from New Directions:

Fresno Stories

Madness in the Family

The Man with the Heart in the Highlands and Other Early Stories

Manufactured in the United States of America

First published as New Directions Paperbook 852 in 1997

Library of Congress Cataloging-in-Publication Data

Saroyan, William, 1908-
[Daring young man on the flying trapeze, and other stories]
The daring young man on the flying trapeze / William Saroyan.
p. cm. — (A New Directions classic)
Originally published: The daring young man on the flying trapeze, and other stories. 1934.
ISBN 13: 978-0-8112-1365-3 (alk. paper)
1. United States—Social life and customs—20th century—Fiction.
2. Armenian Americans—Social life and customs—Fiction. I. Title.
II. Series.
PS3537.A826D3 1997
813' .52—dc21 97-11718
CIP

New Directions Books are published for James Laughlin
by New Directions Publishing Corporation,
80 Eighth Avenue, New York 10011

20 19 18 17 16 15 14 13 12 11

William Saroyan

THE DARING YOUNG MAN ON THE FLYING TRAPEZE

and other stories

A NEW DIRECTIONS CLASSIC

Contents

Preface to the First Edition

I am writing this preface to the first edition so that in the event that this book is issued in a second edition I will be able to write a preface to the second edition, explaining what I said in the preface to the first edition and adding a few remarks about what I have been doing in the meantime, and so on.

In the event that the book reaches a third edition, it is my plan to write a preface to the third edition, covering all that I said in the prefaces to the first and second editions, and it is my plan to go on writing prefaces for new editions of this book until I die. After that I hope there will be children and grandchildren to keep up the good work.

In this early preface, when I have no idea how many copies of the book are going to be sold, the only thing I can do is talk about how I came to write these stories.

Years ago when I was getting a thorough grammar-school education in my home town I found out that stories were something very odd that some sort of men had been turning out (for some odd reason) for hundreds of years, and that there were rules governing the writing of stories.

I immediately began to study all the classic rules, including Ring Lardner's, and in the end I discovered that the rules were wrong.

The trouble was, they had been leaving me out, and as far as I could tell I was the most important element in the matter, so I made some new rules.

I wrote rule Number One when I was eleven and had just been sent home from the fourth grade for having talked out of turn and meant it.

Do not pay any attention to the rules other people make, I wrote. They make them for their own protection, and to hell with them. (I was pretty sore that day.)

Several months later I discovered rule Number Two, which caused a sensation. At any rate, it was a sensation with me. This rule was: Forget Edgar Allan Poe and O. Henry and write the kind of stories you feel like writing. Forget everybody who ever wrote anything.

Since that time I have added four other rules and I have found this number to be enough. Sometimes I do not have to bother about rules at all, and I just sit down and write. Now and then I stand and write.

FIRST EDITION

My third rule was: Learn to typewrite, so you can turn out stories as fast as Zane Grey.

It is one of my best rules.

But rules without a system are, as every good writer will tell you, utterly inadequate. You can leave out "utterly" and the sentence will mean the same thing, but it is always nicer to throw in an "utterly" whenever possible. All successful writers believe that one word by itself hasn't enough meaning and that it is best to emphasize the meaning of one word with the help of another. Some writers will go so far as to help an innocent word with as many as four and five other words, and at times they will kill an innocent word by charity and it will take years and years for some ignorant writer who doesn't know adjectives at all to resurrect the word that was killed by kindness.

Anyway, these stories are the result of a method of composition.

I call it the Festival or Fascist method of composition, and it works this way:

Someone who isn't a writer begins to want to be a writer and he keeps on wanting to be one for ten years, and by that time he has convinced all his relatives and friends and even himself that he *is* a writer, but he hasn't written a thing and he is no longer a boy, so he is getting worried. All he needs now is a system. Some authorities claim there are as many as fifteen systems, but actually there are only two: (1) you can decide to write like Anatole France or Alexandre Dumas or somebody else, or (2) you can decide to forget that you are a writer at all and you can decide to sit down at your typewriter and put words on paper, one at a time, in the best fashion you know how—which brings me to the matter of style.

The matter of style is one that always excites controversy, but to me it is as simple as A B C, if not simpler.

A writer can have, ultimately, one of two styles: he can write in a manner that implies that death is inevitable, or he can write in a manner that implies that death is *not* inevitable. Every style ever employed by a writer has been influenced by one or another of these attitudes toward death.

If you write as if you believe that ultimately you and everyone else alive will be dead, there is a chance that you will write in a pretty earnest style. Otherwise you are apt to be either pompous or soft. On the other hand, in order not to be a fool, you must believe that as much as death is inevitable life is inevitable. That is, the earth is inevitable, and people and other living things on it are inevitable, but that no man can remain on the earth very long. You do not have to be melodramatically tragic about this. As a matter of fact, you can be as amusing as you like about it. It is really one of the basically humorous things, and it has all sorts of possibilities for laughter. If you will remember that living people are as good as dead, you will be able to perceive much that is very funny in their conduct that you perhaps might never have thought of perceiving if you did not believe that they were as good as dead.

The most solid advice, though, for a writer is this, I think: Try to learn to breathe deeply, really to taste food when you eat, and when you sleep, really to sleep. Try as much as possible to be wholly alive, with all your might, and when you laugh, laugh like hell, and when you get angry, get good and angry. Try to be alive. You will be dead soon enough.

The Daring Young Man on the Flying Trapeze

AND OTHER STORIES

The Daring Young Man on the Flying Trapeze

I. SLEEP

Horizontally wakeful amid universal widths, practising laughter and mirth, satire, the end of all, of Rome and yes of Babylon, clenched teeth, remembrance, much warmth volcanic, the streets of Paris, the plains of Jericho, much gliding as of reptile in abstraction, a gallery of watercolors, the sea and the fish with eyes, symphony, a table in the corner of the Eiffel Tower, jazz at the opera house, alarm clock and the tap-dancing of doom, conversation with a tree, the river Nile, Cadillac coupe to Kansas, the roar of Dostoyevsky, and the dark sun.

This earth, the face of one who lived, the form

without the weight, weeping upon snow, white music, the magnified flower twice the size of the universe, black clouds, the caged panther staring, deathless space, Mr. Eliot with rolled sleeves baking bread, Flaubert and Guy de Maupassant, a wordless rhyme of early meaning, Finlandia, mathematics highly polished and slick as a green onion to the teeth, Jerusalem, the path to paradox.

The deep song of man, the sly whisper of someone unseen but vaguely known, hurricane in the cornfield, a game of chess, hush the queen, the king, Karl Franz, black Titanic, Mr. Chaplin weeping, Stalin, Hitler, a multitude of Jews, tomorrow is Monday, no dancing in the streets.

O swift moment of life: it is ended, the earth is again now.

II. WAKEFULNESS

He (the living) dressed and shaved, grinning at himself in the mirror. Very unhandsome, he said; where is my tie? (He had but one.) Coffee and a gray sky, Pacific Ocean fog, the drone of a passing streetcar, people going to the city, time again, the day, prose and poetry. He moved swiftly down the stairs to the street and began to walk, thinking suddenly, *It is only in sleep that we may know that we live. There only, in that living death, do we meet ourselves and the far earth, God and the saints, the names of our fathers, the substance of remote moments; it is there that the centuries merge in the moment, that the vast becomes the tiny, tangible atom of eternity.*

He walked into the day as alertly as might be, making a definite noise with his heels, perceiving with his eyes the superficial truth of streets and structures, the trivial truth of reality. Helplessly his mind sang, *He flies through the air with the greatest of ease; the daring young man on the flying trapeze;* then laughed with all the might of his being. It was really a splendid morning: gray, cold, and cheerless, a morning for inward vigor; ah, Edgar Guest, he said, how I long for your music.

In the gutter he saw a coin which proved to be a penny dated 1923, and placing it in the palm of his hand he examined it closely, remembering that year and thinking of Lincoln whose profile was stamped upon the coin. There was almost nothing a man could do with a penny. I will purchase a motorcar, he thought. I will dress myself in the fashion of a fop, visit the hotel strumpets, drink and dine, and then return to the quiet. Or I will drop the coin into a slot and weigh myself.

It was good to be poor, and the Communists—but it was dreadful to be hungry. What appetites they had, how fond they were of food! Empty stomachs. He remembered how greatly he needed food. Every meal was bread and coffee and cigarettes, and now he had no more bread. Coffee without bread could never honestly serve as supper, and there were no weeds in the park that could be cooked as spinach is cooked.

If the truth were known, he was half starved, and yet there was still no end of books he ought to read before he died. He remembered the young Italian in a Brooklyn hospital, a small sick clerk named Mollica, who had said desperately, I would like to see California once before I die. And he thought earnestly, I ought at least to read *Hamlet* once again; or perhaps *Huckleberry Finn.*

It was then that he became thoroughly awake: at the thought of dying. Now wakefulness was a state in the nature of a sustained shock. A young man could perish rather unostentatiously, he thought; and already he was very nearly starved. Water and prose were fine, they filled much inorganic space, but they were inadequate. If there were only some work he might do for money, some trivial labor in the name of commerce. If they would only allow him to sit at a desk all day and add trade figures, subtract and multiply and divide, then perhaps he would not die. He would buy food, all sorts of it: untasted delicacies from Norway, Italy, and France; all manner of beef, lamb, fish, cheese; grapes, figs, pears, apples, melons, which he would worship when he had satisfied his hunger. He would place a bunch of red grapes on a dish beside two black figs, a large yellow pear, and a green apple. He would hold a cut melòn to his nostrils for hours. He would buy great brown loaves of French bread, vegetables of all sorts, meat; he would buy life.

From a hill he saw the city standing majestically in the east, great towers, dense with his kind, and there he was suddenly outside of it all, almost definitely certain that he should never gain admittance, almost positive that somehow he had ventured upon the wrong earth, or perhaps into the wrong age, and now a young man of twenty-two was to be permanently ejected from it. This thought was not saddening. He said to himself, sometime soon I must write *An Application for Permission to Live.* He accepted the thought of dying without pity for himself or for man, believing that he would at least sleep another night. His rent for another day was paid; there was yet another tomorrow. And after that he might go where other homeless men went. He might even visit the Salvation Army—sing to God and Jesus (unlover of my soul), be saved, eat and sleep. But he knew that he would not. His life was a private life. He did not wish to destroy this fact. Any other alternative would be better.

Through the air on the flying trapeze, his mind hummed. Amusing it was, astoundingly funny. A trapeze to God, or to nothing, a flying trapeze to some sort of eternity; he prayed objectively for strength to make the flight with grace.

I have one cent, he said. It is an American coin. In the evening I shall polish it until it glows like a sun and I shall study the words.

He was now walking in the city itself, among living men. There were one or two places to go. He saw his reflection in the plate-glass windows of stores and was disappointed with his appearance. He seemed not at all as strong as he felt; he seemed, in fact, a trifle infirm in every part of his body, in his neck, his shoulders, arms, trunk, and knees. This will never do, he said, and with an effort he assembled all his disjointed parts and became tensely, artificially erect and solid.

He passed numerous restaurants with magnificent

discipline, refusing even to glance into them, and at last reached a building which he entered. He rose in an elevator to the seventh floor, moved down a hall, and, opening a door, walked into the office of an employment agency. Already there were two dozen young men in the place; he found a corner where he stood waiting his turn to be interviewed. At length he was granted this great privilege and was questioned by a thin, scatterbrained miss of fifty.

Now tell me, she said; what can you do?

He was embarrassed. I can write, he said pathetically.

You mean your penmanship is good? Is that it? said the elderly maiden.

Well, yes, he replied. But I mean that I can write.

Write what? said the miss, almost with anger.

Prose, he said simply.

There was a pause. At last the lady said:

Can you use a typewriter?

Of course, said the young man.

All right, went on the miss, we have your address; we will get in touch with you. There is nothing this morning, nothing at all.

It was much the same at the other agency, except that he was questioned by a conceited young man who closely resembled a pig. From the agencies he went to the large department stores: there was a good deal of pomposity, some humiliation on his part, and finally the report that work was not available. He did not feel displeased, and strangely did not even feel that he was personally involved in all the foolishness. He was a living young man who was in need of money with which to go on being one, and there was no way of getting it except by working for it; and there was no work. It was purely an abstract problem which he wished for the last time to attempt to solve. Now he was pleased that the matter was closed.

He began to perceive the definiteness of the course of his life. Except for moments, it had been largely artless, but now at the last minute he was determined that there should be as little imprecision as possible.

He passed countless stores and restaurants on his way to the Y. M. C. A., where he helped himself to paper and ink and began to compose his *Application*. For an hour he worked on this document, then suddenly, owing to the bad air in the place and to hunger, he became faint. He seemed to be swimming away from himself with great strokes, and hurriedly left the building. In the Civic Center Park, across from the Public Library Building, he drank almost a quart of water and felt himself refreshed. An old man was standing in the center of the brick boulevard surrounded by sea gulls, pigeons, and robins. He was taking handfuls of bread crumbs from a large paper sack and tossing them to the birds with a gallant gesture.

Dimly he felt impelled to ask the old man for a portion of the crumbs, but he did not allow the thought even nearly to reach consciousness; he entered the Public Library and for an hour read Proust, then, feeling himself to be swimming away again, he rushed outdoors. He drank more water at the fountain in the park and began the long walk to his room.

I'll go and sleep some more, he said; there is nothing else to do. He knew now that he was much too tired and weak to deceive himself about being all right, and yet his mind seemed somehow still lithe and alert. It, as if it were a separate entity, persisted in articulating impertinent pleasantries about his very real physical suffering. He reached his room early in the afternoon and immediately prepared coffee on the small gas range. There was no milk in the can, and the half pound of sugar he had purchased a week before was all gone; he drank a cup of the hot black fluid, sitting on his bed and smiling.

From the Y. M. C. A. he had stolen a dozen sheets of letter paper upon which he hoped to complete his document, but now the very notion of writing was unpleasant to him. There was nothing to say. He began to polish the penny he had found in the morning, and this absurd act somehow afforded him great enjoyment. No American coin can be made to shine so brilliantly as a penny. How many pennies would he need to go on living? Wasn't there something more he might sell? He looked about the bare room. No. His watch was gone; also his books. All those fine books; nine of them for eighty-five cents. He felt ill and ashamed for having parted with his books. His best suit he had sold for two dollars, but that was all right. He didn't mind at all about clothes. But the books. That was different. It made him very angry to think that there was no respect for men who wrote.

He placed the shining penny on the table, looking upon it with the delight of a miser. How prettily it smiles, he said. Without reading them he looked at the words, *E Pluribus Unum One Cent United States Of America,* and turning the penny over, he saw Lincoln and the words, *In God We Trust Liberty 1923*. How beautiful it is, he said.

He became drowsy and felt a ghastly illness coming over his blood, a feeling of nausea and disintegration. Bewildered, he stood beside his bed, thinking there *is nothing to do but sleep*. Already he felt himself making great strides through the fluid of the earth, swimming away to the beginning. He fell face down upon the bed, saying, I ought first at least to give the coin to some child. A child could buy any number of things with a penny.

Then swiftly, neatly, with the grace of the young man on the trapeze, he was gone from his body. For an eternal moment he was all things at once: the bird, the fish, the rodent, the reptile, and man. An ocean of print undulated endlessly and darkly before him. The city burned. The herded crowd rioted. The earth circled away, and knowing that he did so, he turned his lost face to the empty sky and became dreamless, unalive, perfect.

Seventy Thousand Assyrians

I hadn't had a haircut in forty days and forty nights, and I was beginning to look like several violinists out of work. You know the look: genius gone to pot, and ready to join the Communist Party. We barbarians from Asia Minor are hairy people: when we need a haircut, we *need* a haircut. It was so bad, I had outgrown my only hat. (I am writing a very serious story, perhaps one of the most serious I shall ever write. That is why I am being flippant. Readers of Sherwood Anderson will begin to understand what I am saying after a while; they will know that my laughter is rather sad.) I was a young man in need of a haircut, so I went down to Third Street (San Francisco), to the Barber College, for a fifteen-cent haircut.

Third Street, below Howard, is a district; think of the Bowery in New York, Main Street in Los Angeles: think of old men and boys, out of work, hanging around, smoking Bull Durham, talking about the government, waiting for something to turn up, simply waiting. It was a Monday morning in August and a lot of the tramps had come to the shop to brighten up a bit. The Japanese boy who was working over the free chair had a waiting list of eleven; all the other chairs were occupied. I sat down and began to wait. Outside, as Hemingway (*The Sun Also Rises; Farewell to Arms; Death in the Afternoon; Winner Take Nothing*) would say, haircuts were four bits. I had twenty cents and a half-pack of Bull Durham. I rolled a cigarette, handed the pack to one of my contemporaries who looked in need of nicotine, and inhaled the dry smoke, thinking of America, what was going on politically, economically, spiritually. My contemporary was a boy of sixteen. He looked Iowa; splendid potentially, a solid American, but down, greatly down in the mouth. Little sleep, no change of clothes for several days, a little fear, etc. I wanted very much to know his name. A writer is always wanting to get the reality of faces and figures. Iowa said, "I just got in from Salinas. No work in the lettuce fields. Going north now, to Portland; try to ship out." I wanted to tell him how it was with me: rejected story from *Scribner's*, rejected essay from *The Yale Review*, no money for decent cigarettes, worn shoes, old shirts, but I was afraid to make something of my own troubles. A writer's troubles are always boring, a bit unreal. People are apt to feel, *Well, who asked you to write in the first place?* A man must pretend not to be a writer. I said, "Good luck, north." Iowa shook his head. "I know better. Give it a try, anyway. Nothing to lose." Fine boy, hope he isn't dead, hope he hasn't frozen, mighty cold these days (December, 1933), hope he hasn't gone down; he deserved to live. Iowa, I hope you got work in Portland; I hope you are earning money; I hope you have rented a clean room with a warm bed in it; I hope you are sleeping nights, eating regularly, walking along like a human being, being happy. Iowa, my good wishes are with you. I have said a number of prayers for you. (All the same, I think he is dead by this time. It was in him the day I saw him, the low malicious face of the beast, and at the same time all the theatres in America were showing, over and over again, an animated film-cartoon in which there was a song called "Who's Afraid of the Big Bad Wolf?", and that's what it amounts to; people with money laughing at the death that is crawling slyly into boys like young Iowa, pretending that it isn't there, laughing in warm theatres. I have prayed for Iowa, and I consider myself a coward. By this time he must be dead, and I am sitting in a small room, talking about him, only talking.)

I began to watch the Japanese boy who was learning to become a barber. He was shaving an old tramp who had a horrible face, one of those faces that emerge from years and years of evasive living, years of being unsettled, of not belonging anywhere, of owning nothing, and the Japanese boy was holding his nose back (his own nose) so that he would not smell the old tramp. A trivial point in a story, a bit of data with no place in a work of art, nevertheless, I put it down. A young writer is always afraid some significant fact may escape him. He is always wanting to put in everything he sees. I wanted to know the name of the Japanese boy. I am profoundly interested in names. I have found that those that are unknown are the most genuine. Take a big name like Andrew Mellon. I was watching the Japanese boy very closely. I wanted to understand from the way he was keeping his sense of smell away from the mouth and nostrils of the old man what he was thinking, how he was feeling. Years ago, when I was seventeen, I pruned vines in my uncle's vineyard, north of Sanger, in the San Joaquin Valley, and there were several Japanese working with me, Yoshio Enomoto, Hideo Suzuki, Katsumi Sujimoto, and one or two others. These Japanese taught me a few simple phrases, *hello, how are you, fine day, isn't it, good-bye,* and so on. I said in Japanese to the barber student, "How are you?" He said in Japanese, "Very well, thank you." Then, in impeccable English, "Do you speak Japanese? Have you lived in Japan?" I said, "Unfortunately, no. I am able to speak only one or two words. I used to work with Yoshio Enomoto, Hideo Suzuki, Katsumi Sujimoto; do you know them?" He went on with his work, thinking of the names. He seemed to be whispering, "Enomoto, Suzuki, Sujimoto." He said, "Suzuki. Small man?" I said, "Yes." He said, "I know him. He lives in San Jose now. He is married now."

I want you to know that I am deeply interested in what people remember. A young writer goes out to places and talks to people. He tries to find out what they remember. I am not using great material for a short story. Nothing is going to happen in this work. I am not fabricating a fancy plot. I am not creating memorable characters. I am not using a slick style of writing. I am not building up a fine atmosphere. I have no desire to sell this story or any story to *The Saturday Evening Post* or to *Cosmopolitan* or to *Harper's*. I am not trying to compete with the great writers of short stories, men like Sinclair Lewis and Joseph Hergesheimer and Zane Grey, men who really know how to write, how to make up stories that will sell. Rich men, men who understand all the rules about plot and character and style and atmosphere and all that stuff. I have no desire for fame. I am not out to win the Pulitzer Prize or the Nobel Prize or any other prize. I am out here in the far West, in San Francisco, in a small room on Carl Street, writing a letter to common people, telling them in simple language things they already know. I am merely making a record, so if I wander around a little, it is because I am in no hurry and because I do not know the rules. If I have any desire at all, it is to show the brotherhood of man. This is a big statement and it sounds a little precious. Generally a man is ashamed to make such a statement. He is afraid sophisticated people will laugh at him. But I don't mind. I'm asking sophisticated people to laugh. That is what sophistication is for. I do not believe in races. I do not believe in governments. I see life as one life at one time, so many millions simultaneously, all over the earth. Babies who have not yet been taught to speak any language are the only race of the earth, the race of man: all the rest is pretense, what we call civilization, hatred, fear, desire for strength. . . . But a baby is a baby. And the way they cry, there you have the brotherhood of man, babies crying. We grow up and we learn the words of a language and we see the universe through the language we know, we do not see it through all languages or through no language at all, through silence, for example, and we isolate ourselves in the language we know. Over here we isolate ourselves in English, or American as Mencken calls it. All the eternal things, in our words. If I want to do anything, I want to speak a more universal language. The heart of man, the unwritten part of man, that which is eternal and common to all races.

Now I am beginning to feel guilty and incompetent. I have used all this language and I am beginning to feel that I have said nothing. This is what drives a young writer out of his head, this feeling that nothing is being said. Any ordinary journalist would have been able to put the whole business into a three-word caption. Man is man, he would have said. Something clever, with any number of implications. But I want to use language that will create a single implication. I want the meaning to be precise, and perhaps that is why the language is so imprecise. I am walking around my subject, the impression I want to make, and I am trying to see it from all angles, so that I will have a whole picture, a picture of wholeness. It is the heart of man that I am trying to imply in this work.

Let me try again: I hadn't had a haircut in a long time and I was beginning to look seedy, so I went down to the Barber College on Third Street, and I sat in a chair. I said, "Leave it full in the back. I have a narrow head and if you do not leave it full in the back, I will go out of this place looking like a horse. Take as much as you like off the top. No lotion, no water, comb it dry." Reading makes a full man, writing a precise one, as you see. This is what happened. It doesn't make much of a story, and the reason is that I have left out the barber, the young man who gave me the haircut.

He was tall, he had a dark serious face, thick lips, on the verge of smiling but melancholy, thick lashes, sad eyes, a large nose. I saw his name on the card that was pasted on the mirror, Theodore Badal. A good name, genuine, a good young man, genuine. Theodore Badal began to work on my head. A good barber never speaks until he has been spoken to, no matter how full his heart may be.

"That name," I said, "Badal. Are you an Armenian?" I am an Armenian. I have mentioned this before. People look at me and begin to wonder, so I come right out and tell them. "I am an Armenian," I say. Or they read something I have written and begin to wonder, so I let them know. "I am an Armenian," I say. It is a meaningless remark, but they expect me to say it, so I do. I have no idea what it is like to be an Armenian or what it is like to be an

Englishman or a Japanese or anything else. I have a faint idea what it is like to be alive. This is the only thing that interests me greatly. This and tennis. I hope some day to write a great philosophical work on tennis, something on the order of *Death in the Afternoon,* but I am aware that I am not yet ready to undertake such a work. I feel that the cultivation of tennis on a large scale among the peoples of the earth will do much to annihilate racial differences, prejudices, hatred, etc. Just as soon as I have perfected my drive and my lob, I hope to begin my outline of this great work. (It may seem to some sophisticated people that I am trying to make fun of Hemingway. I am not. *Death in the Afternoon* is a pretty sound piece of prose. I could never object to it as prose. I cannot even object to it as philosophy. I think it is finer philosophy than that of Will Durant and Walter Pitkin. Even when Hemingway is a fool, he is at least an accurate fool. He tells you what actually takes place and he doesn't allow the speed of an occurrence to make his exposition of it hasty. This is a lot. It is some sort of advancement for literature. To relate leisurely the nature and meaning of that which is very brief in duration.)

"Are you an Armenian?" I asked.

We are a small people and whenever one of us meets another, it is an event. We are always looking around for someone to talk to in our language. Our most ambitious political party estimates that there are nearly two million of us living on the earth, but most of us don't think so. Most of us sit down and take a pencil and a piece of paper and we take one section of the world at a time and imagine how many Armenians at the most are likely to be living in that section and we put the highest number on the paper, and then we go on to another section, India, Russia, Soviet Armenia, Egypt, Italy, Germany, France, America, South America, Australia, and so on, and after we add up our most hopeful figures the total comes to something a little less than a million. Then we start to think how big our families are, how high our birth-rate and how low our death-rate (except in times of war when massacres increase the death-rate), and we begin to imagine how rapidly we will increase if we are left alone a quarter of a century, and we feel pretty happy. We always leave out earthquakes, wars, massacres, famines, etc., and it is a mistake. I remember the Near East Relief drives in my home town. My uncle used to be our orator and he used to make a whole auditorium full of Armenians weep. He was an attorney and he was a great orator. Well, at first the trouble was war. Our people were being destroyed by the enemy. Those who hadn't been killed were homeless and they were starving, *our own flesh and blood,* my uncle said, and we all wept. And we gathered money and sent it to our people in the old country. Then after the war, when I was a bigger boy, we had another Near East Relief drive and my uncle stood on the stage of the Civic Auditorium of my home town and he said, "Thank God this time it is not the enemy, but an earthquake. God has made us suffer. We have worshipped Him through trial and tribulation, through suffering and disease and torture and horror and (my uncle began to weep, began to sob) through the madness of despair, and now he has done this thing, and still we praise Him, still we worship Him. We do not understand the ways of God." And after the drive I went to my uncle and I said, "Did you mean what you said about God?" And he said, "That was oratory. We've got to raise money. What God? It is nonsense." "And when you cried?" I asked, and my uncle said, "That was real. I could not help it. I had to cry. Why, for God's sake, why must we go through all this God damn hell? What have we done to deserve all this torture? Man won't let us alone. God won't let us alone. Have we done something? Aren't we supposed to be pious people? What is our sin? I am disgusted with God. I am sick of man. The only reason I am willing to get up and talk is that I don't dare keep my mouth shut. I can't bear the thought of more of our people dying. Jesus Christ, have we done something?"

I asked Theodore Badal if he was an Armenian.

He said, "I am an Assyrian."

Well, it was something. They, the Assyrians, came from our part of the world, they had noses like our noses, eyes like our eyes, hearts like our hearts. They had a different language. When they spoke we couldn't understand them, but they were a lot like us. It wasn't quite as pleasing as it would have been if Badal had been an Armenian, but it was something.

"I am an Armenian," I said. "I used to know some Assyrian boys in my home town, Joseph Sargis, Nito Elia, Tony Saleh. Do you know any of them?"

"Joseph Sargis, I know him," said Badal. "The others I do not know. We lived in New York until five years ago, then we came out west to Turlock. Then we moved up to San Francisco."

"Nito Elia," I said, "is a Captain in the Salvation Army." (I don't want anyone to imagine that I am making anything up, or that I am trying to be funny.) "Tony Saleh," I said, "was killed eight years ago. He was riding a horse and he was thrown and the horse began to run. Tony couldn't get himself free, he was caught by a leg, and the horse ran around and around for a half hour and then stopped, and when they went up to Tony he was dead. He was fourteen at the time. I used to go to school with him. Tony was a very clever boy, very good at arithmetic."

We began to talk about the Assyrian language and the Armenian language, about the old world, conditions over there, and so on. I was getting a fifteen-cent haircut and I was doing my best to learn something at the same time, to acquire some new truth, some new appreciation of the wonder of life, the dignity of man. (Man has great dignity, do not imagine that he has not.)

Badal said, "I cannot read Assyrian. I was born in the old country, but I want to get over it."

He sounded tired, not physically but spiritually.

"Why?" I said. "Why do you want to get over it?"

"Well," he laughed, "simply because everything is washed up over there." I am repeating his words precisely, putting in nothing of my own. "We were a great people once," he went on. "But that was yesterday, the day before yesterday. Now we are a topic in ancient history. We had a great civilization. They're still admiring it. Now I am in America learning how to cut hair. We're washed up as a race, we're through, it's all over, why should I learn to read the language? We have no writers, we have no news—well, there is a little news: once in a while the English encourage the Arabs to massacre us, that is all. It's an old story, we know all about it. The news comes over to us through the Associated Press, anyway."

These remarks were very painful to me, an Armenian. I had always felt badly about my own people being destroyed. I had never heard an Assyrian speaking in English about such things. I felt great love for this young fellow. Don't get me wrong. There is a tendency these days to think in terms of pansies whenever a man says that he has affection for man. I think now that I have affection for all people, even for the enemies of Armenia, whom I have so tactfully not named. Everyone knows who they are. I have nothing against any of them because I think of them as one man living one life at a time, and I know, I am positive, that one man at a time is incapable of the monstrosities performed by mobs. My objection is to mobs only.

"Well," I said, "it is much the same with us. We, too, are old. We still have our church. We still have a few writers, Aharonian, Isahakian, a few others, but it is much the same."

"Yes," said the barber, "I know. We went in for the wrong things. We went in for the simple things, peace and quiet and families. We didn't go in for machinery and conquest and militarism. We didn't go in for diplomacy and deceit and the invention of machine-guns and poison gases. Well, there is no use in being disappointed. We had our day, I suppose."

"We are hopeful," I said. "There is no Armenian living who does not still dream of an independent Armenia."

"Dream?" said Badal. "Well, that is something. Assyrians cannot even dream any more. Why, do you know how many of us are left on earth?"

"Two or three million," I suggested.

"Seventy thousand," said Badal. "That is all. Seventy thousand Assyrians in the world, and the Arabs are still killing us. They killed seventy of us in a little uprising last month. There was a small paragraph in the paper. Seventy more of us destroyed. We'll be wiped out before long. My brother is married to an American girl and he has a son. There is no more hope. We are trying to forget Assyria. My father still reads a paper that comes from New York, but he is an old man. He will be dead soon."

Then his voice changed, he ceased speaking as an Assyrian and began to speak as a barber: "Have I taken enough off the top?" he asked.

The rest of the story is pointless. I said *so long* to the young Assyrian and left the shop. I walked across town, four miles, to my room on Carl Street. I thought about the whole business: Assyria and this Assyrian, Theodore Badal, learning to be a barber, the sadness of his voice, the hopelessness of his attitude. This was months ago, in August, but ever since I have been thinking about Assyria, and I have been wanting to say something about Theodore Badal, a son of an ancient race, himself youthful and alert, yet hopeless. Seventy thousand Assyrians, a mere seventy thousand of that great people, and all the others quiet in death and all the greatness crumbled and ignored, and a young man in America learning to be a barber, and a young man lamenting bitterly the course of history.

Why don't I make up plots and write beautiful love stories that can be made into motion pictures? Why don't I let these unimportant and boring matters go hang? Why don't I try to please the American reading public?

Well, I am an Armenian. Michael Arlen is an Armenian, too. He is pleasing the public. I have great admiration for him, and I think he has perfected a very fine style of writing and all that, but I don't want to write about the people he likes to write about. Those people were dead to begin with. You take Iowa and the Japanese boy and Theodore Badal, the Assyrian; well, they may go down physically, like Iowa, to death, or spiritually, like Badal, to death, but they are of the stuff that is eternal in man and it is this stuff that interests me. You don't find them in bright places, making witty remarks about sex and trivial remarks about art. You find them where I found them, and they will be there forever, the race of man, the part of man, of Assyria as much as of England, that cannot be destroyed, the part that massacre does not destroy, the part that earthquake and war and famine and madness and everything else cannot destroy.

This work is in tribute to Iowa, to Japan, to Assyria, to Armenia, to the race of man everywhere, to the dignity of that race, the brotherhood of things alive. I am not expecting Paramount Pictures to film this work. I am thinking of seventy thousand Assyrians, one at a time, alive, a great race. I am thinking of Theodore Badal, himself seventy thousand Assyrians and seventy million Assyrians, himself Assyria, and man, standing in a barber shop, in San Francisco, in 1933, and being, still, himself, the whole race.

Among the Lost

At a table in a far corner of the room Paul smoked a cigarette, looking into *New Bearings in English Poetry,* absorbing random phrases, *accuse him of sentimental evasions . . . meditations upon a deterministic universe. . . . Hardy's great poetry . . . the impulse . . . Ezra Pound . . . Hugh Selwyn Mauberly. . . .*

He slipped the small book into his coat pocket and walked beyond the swinging doors, into Number One Opera Alley. Red, the bookie-clerk was telling a fellow how once, three years ago, he had been stabbed by a crazy Russian who had lost twenty dollars on the ponies. A month in the hospital, Red said. We didn't prosecute because it would have given the "Kentucky" a bad name. The Russian cried and said he would never come down to Third Street again, so we let it go at that. For a while they thought I was going to die.

He grinned tightly, smiling. This place is like home, he said. The boys caught him at the *Examiner* corner. My friends, all the boys who know me. They were going to kill him.

Red looked around to see if anyone was listening. Do you know, he said, when I was in the hospital I worried about that crazy Russian? He came into this place all of a sudden and started to make bets, the craziest bets you ever did see a man make, long shots, impossible horses. I told him once or twice to take it easy, but he was out to make a killing. Then he went broke and sat on that bench over there, looking at me. I could tell he was going nuts, but I didn't know he had a knife. I thought he might make a pass at me and I would let him have one on the chin. When the races were over and all the fellows had beat it, he was still sitting on the bench, looking at me. Then I *knew* he was nuts. He got me right below the heart, but do you know, after he had stuck the knife in me, I began to worry about him. I had an idea I would get over the wound all right, but this nut, this Russian, the way he looked after he had done it. He began to jabber in Russian, and then he beat it down the alley, with Pat and Brown chasing him.

Paul went over to Red. You never told me that

story, he said. What did you think, right after he stabbed you?

I didn't think anything, Red said. I began to swear because I had planned to go out to the beach with my wife that night. It made me sore because I wouldn't be able to go out to the beach. I knew it was a cut that would send me to the hospital, and I began to swear.

Through the swinging doors Paul returned to the table in the corner, waiting for Lambough. Smithy, whose neck was as fat as his head, walked among the card tables, crying out every now and then, Seat here for a player . . . one more seat. Paul watched the men coming and going, counting their nickels, talking to themselves, the way it is with petty gamblers. He opened the book again, coming upon *existlessness, modulation, shift of stress and rhyme.* Then he rose and sauntered about the room, studying the men and remembering fragments of their talk. *There is a horse in the seventh at Latonia, Dark Sea. I like Foxhall. Yesterday, three winners, but I was broke. A small fortune.*

The small Irish waiter, called Alabama, was carrying coffee to a table, looking dully at nothing and asking: How many sugars?

Paul stood in the smoke, waiting for Lambough. It was almost eleven and the appointment was for ten-thirty. Paul handed his package of cigarettes to a thin consumptive Jew. Take several, he suggested, and the Jew smiled and asked how it had been with Paul.

Graceless, said Paul. The Jew groaned and lit a cigarette.

I sell flowers in the streets, he said, and there is a law against it. Saturday night they took me to jail. I just got out. Two nights. I couldn't eat. I couldn't sleep. I felt dirty. All night the men yell. Is it wrong to sell flowers?

Hardly, said Paul. Tell me about the jail.

He led the way to the table in the corner, and the Jew sat across from him.

It is not for us, that place, the Jew said. They put me in a cesspool with three others. One was a beggar. I don't know what the others were, but they looked bad. I don't mean they were criminals. Bad, they themselves. All night I felt like a man in a room with frogs, warty things, and I kept holding the door and crying. I am ashamed. It is not often that I cry, but it was rotten. In another cell . . . but it is too rotten.

Go ahead, said Paul. I've never been in jail. Tell me what it is like.

In the next room, said the Jew, were two pansies. And the other two men, they were talking to those fellows . . . I mean whispering and begging, and the pansies were saying *no,* just like cheap women. I didn't know men were really that way. I thought it was just talk, joking. And in all the rooms was that dirty laughter. I was sick all the time, and I had no cigarettes.

What food did they bring you? Paul asked.

Slop . . . dirt . . .

Bread?

Yes, bread, but I couldn't eat. Only the bread was fit to eat, but I was too sick.

Do you remember any of the things the men said at night? Did they sing?

Yes, said the Jew.

Any religious songs?

Yes, religious, with dirty words.

Did anyone pray?

I heard only cussing, said the Jew.

Across the room Paul saw Lambough walking slowly, holding a copy of the morning paper. He came soberly to the table and sat down without a word.

This man just got out of jail, Paul said. He sells flowers. They put him in Saturday.

Lambough glanced at the Jew and asked him if he felt all right. It seemed to him that the Jew must be very ill.

I feel better, the Jew said. Anything is better than that place.

What are you going to do? Lambough asked.

The Jew coughed. I'll try again. If they catch me, I don't know what I'll do. I can't beg.

Paul said to Lambough, How much money have we?

I've got sixty cents, Lambough said.

The Jew got to his feet. Thanks for the cigarettes, he said to Paul.

We're almost broke, Paul said. Can you use a quarter?

He brought some small change from his pants pocket.

Thanks, said the Jew. I'll try again. If they come after me, I'll run.

He hurried away from the table in confusion. Lambough watched him walk away. Everybody around here is either sick or cracked, he said. That poor fellow is ready to keel. What'd he say?

Nearly killed him, the jail, said Paul.

I went up to a place on Jones Street, said Lambough. They had an ad in the paper for a student to work for room and board. I didn't get the job.

But you *are* a student, said Paul. You had a right to go up. By the way, what *are* you studying?

Starvation, said Lambough. Sure I'm a student. I felt lucky not to get the job, though. It was a cheap rooming house. They hired a Willy from Manila.

What's on your mind? Paul asked.

Nothing, as usual, said Lambough. I'm just killing time.

Do you think we'll ever get jobs?

Oh, said Lambough, it's a cinch.

So it looks bad, said Paul.

Well, said Lambough, it doesn't look good. Everything looks the same as ever, only more well-dressed men are begging in the streets. I had a talk with that girl up on Eddy Street. We get to sleep in the waiting-room again if business is slow.

How was she? said Paul.

Who? said Lambough. The girl? Oh, fine; she looked all right.

What can you think of to talk about? Paul asked.

You know me, said Lambough. One thing or the next. I know a little about everything.

Paul slipped *New Bearings in English Poetry* from his coat pocket. What do you know about English poetry? he asked Lambough.

What? said Lambough. You don't want to go on discussing economics?

Nuts, said Paul. We covered all that.

Yes, said Lambough, but what has English poetry got to do with us?

Nothing has anything much to do with us, said Paul. We're a bit out of the picture at the moment. So you don't know anything about English poetry? Did you ever hear of T. S. Eliot?

No, said Lambough. What about him?

Well, said Paul, he is a pretty fine poet.

Well, what of it? said Lambough. Who cares?

I mean, said Paul, if you knew something about him, we could talk and kill time. As it is, tell me about Ireland. You're Irish, aren't you?

Sure I'm Irish, said Lambough, but what the hell, I was born in Kansas. I've never seen Ireland.

All right, said Paul. Tell me how you imagine Ireland to be. It's a long time till midnight. We've got to talk about something. Ireland is a good subject.

He began to listen to Lambough explaining that he knew nothing about Ireland, except maybe what he had gathered from Irish songs, most of them written in America by Jews and others. Once every year, he thought, while Lambough talked, to be among the lost, to know how it feels to be out of things, to have no present, no future, to belong nowhere, to be suspended between day and night, waiting.

At midnight, he thought, I will go with this boy

to that waiting-room and try to sleep in a chair, Smithy shouting, Seat here for a player . . . one more seat, and the petty gamblers coming and going, Lambough talking in the morning about Ireland, the sick Jew in jail, Red stabbed by the crazy Russian, sentimental evasions, *the winter evening settles down with smell of steaks in passageways,* meditations upon a deterministic universe, *the readers of the Boston Evening Transcript,* the impulse, *when Mr. Apollinax visited the United States his laughter tinkled among the teacups,* the day dwindling amid talk, the country perishing, all the young men waiting, hunger marches, *as she laughed I was aware of becoming involved in her laughter,* Ezra Pound, the American in France, *an old man in a dry month, being read to by a boy, waiting for rain, defunctive music under sea, the smoky candle end of time declines,* democratic progress, the Jew in jail, holding the door and crying, *in the beginning was the Word, for Ezra Pound il miglior fabbro,* the small Jew weeping, a flower peddler among beggars and homo-sexuals, meditations amid the smoke and ruins of a deterministic universe, the crazy Russian running down Opera Alley, and Red bleeding, *wipe your hand across your mouth, and laugh,* and laugh, and laugh, the little Jew standing in the filth, holding the door and weeping, everyone waiting everywhere, *there will be time to murder and create, and indeed there will be time,* there will be time, a young man listening to the talk of another young man, waiting for national recovery, *time to murder and create.*

Myself upon the Earth

A beginning is always difficult, for it is no simple matter to choose from language the one bright word which shall live forever; and every articulation of the solitary man is but a single word. Every poem, story, novel and essay, just as every dream is a word from that language we have not yet translated, that vast unspoken wisdom of night, that grammarless, lawless vocabulary of eternity. The earth is vast. And with the earth all things are vast, the skyscraper and the blade of grass. The eye will magnify if the mind and soul will allow. And the mind may destroy time, brother of death, and brother, let us remember, of life as well. Vastest of all is the ego, the germ of humanity, from which is born God and the universe, heaven and hell, the earth, the face of man, my face and your face; our eyes. For myself, I say with piety, rejoice.

I am a young man in an old city. It is morning and I am in a small room. I am standing over a bundle of yellow writing paper, the only sort of paper I can afford, the kind that sells at the rate of one hundred and seventy sheets for ten cents. All this paper is bare of language, clean and perfect, and I am a young writer about to begin my work. It is Monday . . . September 25, 1933 . . . how glorious it is to be alive, to be still living. (I am an old man; I have walked along many streets, through many cities, through many days and many nights. And now I have come home to myself. Over me, on the wall of this small, disordered room, is the photograph of my dead father, and I have come up from the earth with his face and his eyes and I am writing in English what he would have written in our native tongue. And we are the same man, one dead and one alive.) Furiously I am smoking a cigarette, for the moment is one of great importance to me, and therefore of great importance to everyone. I am about to place language, my language, upon a clean sheet of paper, and I am trembling. It is so much of a responsibility to be a user of words. I do not want to say the wrong thing. I do not want to be clever. I am horribly afraid of this. I have never been clever in life, and now that I have come to a labor even more magnificent than living itself I do not want to utter a single false word. For months I have been telling myself, "You must be humble. Above all things, you must be humble." I am determined not to lose my character.

I am a story-teller, and I have but a single story—man. I want to tell this simple story in my own way, forgetting the rules of rhetoric, the tricks of composition. I have something to say and I do not wish to speak like Balzac. I am not an artist; I do not really believe in civilization. I am not at all enthusiastic about progress. When a great bridge is built I do not cheer, and when airplanes cross the Atlantic I do not think, "What a marvelous age this is!" I am not interested in the destiny of nations, and history bores me. What do they mean by history, those who write it and believe in it? How has it happened that man, that humble and lovable creature, has been exploited for the purpose of monstrous documents? How has it happened that his solitude has been destroyed, his godliness herded into a hideous riot of murder and destruction? And I do not believe in commerce. I regard all machinery as junk, the adding-machine, the automobile, the railway engine, the airplane, yes, and the bicycle. I do not believe in transportation, in going places with the body, and I would like to know where anyone has ever gone. Have you ever left yourself? Is any journey so vast and interesting as the journey of the mind through life? Is the end of any journey so beautiful as death?

I am interested only in man. Life I love, and before death I am humble. I cannot fear death because it is purely physical. Is it not true that today both I and my father are living, and that in my flesh is assembled all the past of man? But I despise violence and I hate bitterly those who perpetrate and practise it. The injury of a living man's small finger I regard as infinitely more disastrous and ghastly than his natural death. And when multitudes of men are hurt to death in wars I am driven to a grief which borders on insanity. I become impotent with rage. My only weapon is language, and while I know it is stronger than machine-guns, I despair because I cannot single-handed annihilate the notion of destruction which propagandists awaken in men. I myself, however, am a propagandist, and in this very story I am trying to restore man to his natural dignity and gentleness. I want to restore man to himself. I want to send him from the mob to his own body and mind. I want to lift him from the nightmare of history to the calm dream of his own soul, the true chronicle of his kind. I want him to be himself. It is proper only to herd cattle. When the spirit of a single man is taken from him and he is made a member of a mob, the body of God suffers a ghastly pain, and therefore the act is a blasphemy.

I am opposed to mediocrity. If a man is an honest idiot, I can love him, but I cannot love a dishonest genius. All my life I have laughed at rules and mocked traditions, styles and mannerisms. How can a rule be applied to such a wonderful invention as man? Every life is a contradiction, a new truth, a new miracle, and even frauds are interesting. I am not a philosopher and I do not believe in philosophies; the word itself I look upon with suspicion. I believe in the right of man to contradict himself. For instance, did I not say that I look upon machinery as junk, and yet do I not worship the typewriter? Is it not the dearest possession I own?

And now I am coming to the little story I set out to tell. It is about myself and my typewriter, and it is perhaps a trivial story. You can turn to any of the national five-cent magazines and find much more artful stories, stories of love and passion and despair and ecstasy, stories about men called Elmer Fowler, Wilfred Diggens, and women called Florence Farwell, Agatha Hume, and so on.

If you turn to these magazines, you will find any number of perfect stories, full of plot, atmosphere, mood, style, character, and all those other things a good story is supposed to have, just as good mayonnaise is supposed to have so much pure olive oil, so much cream, and so much whipping. (Please do not imagine that I have forgotten myself and that I am trying to be clever. I am not laughing at these stories. I am not laughing at the people who read them. These words of prose and the men and women and children who read them constitute one of the most touching documents of our time, just as the motion pictures of Hollywood and those who spend the greatest portion of their secret lives watching them constitute one of the finest sources of material for the honest novelist. Invariably, let me explain, when I visit the theatre, and it is rarely that I have the price of admission, I am profoundly moved by the flood of emotion which surges from the crowd, and newsreels have always brought hot tears from my eyes. I cannot see floods, tornadoes, fires, wars and the faces of politicians without weeping. Even the tribulations of Mickey Mouse make my heart bleed, for I know that he, artificial as he may be, is actually a symbol of man.) Therefore, do not misunderstand me. I am not a satirist. There is actually nothing to satire, and everything pathetic or fraudulent contains its own mockery. I wish to point out merely that I am a writer, a story-teller. I go on writing as if all the periodicals in the country were clamoring for my work, offering me vast sums of money for anything I might choose to say. I sit in my room smoking one cigarette after another, writing this story of mine, which I know will never be able to meet the stiff competition of my more artful and talented contemporaries. Is it not strange? And why should I, a story-teller, be so attached to my typewriter? What earthly good is it to me? And what satisfaction do I get from writing stories?

Well, that is the story. Still, I do not want anyone to suppose that I am complaining. I do not want you to feel that I am a hero of some sort, or, on the other hand, that I am a sentimentalist. I am actually neither of these things. I have no objection to *The Saturday Evening Post,* and I do not believe the editor of *Scribner's* is a fool because he will not publish my tales. I know precisely what every magazine in the country wants. I know the sort of material *Secret Stories* is seeking, and the sort *The American Mercury* prefers, and the sort preferred by the literary journals like *Hound & Horn,* and all the rest. I read all magazines and I know what sort of stuff will sell. Still, I am seldom published and poor. Is it that I cannot write the sort of stuff for which money is paid?

I assure you that it is not. I can write any sort of story you can think of. If Edgar Rice Burroughs were to die this morning, I could go on writing about Tarzan and the Apes. Or if I felt inclined, I could write like John Dos Passos or William Faulkner or James Joyce. (And so could you, for that matter.)

But I have said that I want to preserve my identity. Well, I mean it. If in doing this it is essential for me to remain unpublished, I am satisfied. I do not believe in fame. It is a form of fraudulence, and any famous man will tell you so. Any honest man, at any rate. How can one living man possibly be greater than another? And what difference does it make if one man writes great novels which are printed and another writes great novels which are not? What has the printing of novels to do with their greatness? What has money or the lack of it to do with the character of a man?

But I will confess that you've got to be proud and religious to be the sort of writer that I am. You've got to have an astounding amount of strength. And it takes years and years to become the sort of writer that I am, sometimes centuries. I wouldn't advise any young man with a talent for words to try to write the way I do. I would suggest that he study Theodore Dreiser or Sinclair Lewis. I would suggest even that, rather than attempt my method, he follow in the footsteps of O. Henry or the contributors to *The Woman's Home Companion.* Because, briefly, I am not a writer at all. I have been laughing at the rules of writing ever since I started to write, ten, maybe fifteen, years ago. I am simply a young man. I write because there is nothing more civilized or decent for me to do.

Do you know that I do not believe there is really such a thing as a poem-form, a story-form or a novel-form? I believe there is man only. The rest is trickery. I am trying to carry over into this story of mine the man that I am. And as much of my earth as I am able. I want more than anything else to be honest and fearless in my own way. Do you think I could not, if I chose, omit the remark I made about Dos Passos and Faulkner and Joyce, a remark which is both ridiculous and dangerous? Why, if someone were to say to me, "All right, you say you can write like Faulkner, well, then, let's see you do it." If someone were to say this to me, I would be positively stumped and I would have to admit timidly that I couldn't do the trick. Nevertheless, I make the statement and let it stand. And what is more, no one can prove that I am cracked; I could make the finest alienist in Vienna seem a raving maniac to his own disciples, or if I did not prefer this course, I could act as dull and stupid and sane as a Judge of the Supreme Court. Didn't I say that in my flesh is gathered all the past of man? And surely there have been dolts in that past.

I do not know, but there may be a law of some sort against this kind of writing. It may be a misdemeanor. I hope so. It is impossible for me to smash a fly which has tickled my nose, or to step on an ant, or to hurt the feelings of any man, idiot or genius, but I cannot resist the temptation to mock any law which is designed to hamper the spirit of man. It is essential for me to stick pins in pompous balloons. I love to make small explosions with the inflated bags of moralists, cowards, and wise men. Listen and you will hear such a small explosion in this paragraph.

All this rambling may seem pointless and a waste of time, but it is not. There is absolutely no haste—I can walk the hundred yard dash in a full day—and anyone who prefers may toss this story aside and take up something in the *Cosmopolitan*. I am not asking anyone to stand by. I am not promising golden apples to all who are patient. I am sitting in my room, living my life, tapping my typewriter. I am sitting in the presence of my father, who has been gone from the earth so many years. Every two or three minutes I look up into his melancholy face to see how he is taking it all. It is like looking into a mirror, for I see myself. I am almost as old as he was when the photograph was taken and I am wearing the very same moustache he wore at the time. I worship this man. All my life I have worshipped him. When both of us lived on the earth I was much too young to exchange so much as a single word with him, consciously, but ever since I have come to consciousness and articulation we have had many long silent conversations. I say to him, "Ah, you melancholy Armenian, you; how marvelous your life has been!" And he replies gently, "Be humble, my son. Seek God."

My father was a writer, too. He was an unpublished writer. I have all his great manuscripts, his great poems and stories, written in our native language, which I cannot read. Two or three times each year I bring out all my father's papers and stare for hours at his contribution to the literature of the world. Like myself, I am pleased to say, he was desperately poor; poverty trailed him like a hound, as the expression is. Most of his poems and stories were written on wrapping paper which he folded into small books. Only his journal is in English (which he spoke and wrote perfectly), and it is full of lamentations. In New York, according to this journal, my father had only two moods: *sad* and *very sad*. About thirty years ago he was alone in that city, and he was trying to earn enough money to pay for the passage of his wife and three children to the new world. He was a janitor. Why should I withhold this fact? There is nothing shameful about a great man's being a janitor in America. In the old country he was a man of honor, a professor, and he was called Agha, which means approximately lord. Unfortunately, he was also a revolutionist, as all good Armenians are. He wanted the handful of people of his race to be free. He wanted them to enjoy liberty, and so he was placed in jail every now and then. Finally, it got so bad that if he did not leave the old country, he would kill and be killed. He knew English, he had read Shakespeare and Swift in English, and so he came to this country. And they made a janitor of him. After a number of years of hard work his family joined him in New York. In California, according to my father's journal, matters for a while were slightly better for him; he mentioned sunshine and magnificent bunches of grapes. So he tried farming. At first he worked for other farmers, then he made a down payment on a small farm of his own. But he was a rotten farmer. He was a man of books, a professor; he loved good clothes. He loved leisure and comfort, and like myself he hated machinery.

My father's vineyard was about eleven miles east of the nearest town, and all the farmers near by were in the habit of going to town once or twice a week on bicycles, which were the vogue at that time and a trifle faster than a horse and buggy. One hot afternoon in August a tall individual in very fine clothes was seen moving forward in long leisurely strides over a hot and dusty country road. It was my father. My people told me this story about the man, so that I might understand what a fool he was and not be like him. Someone saw my father. It was a neighbor farmer who was returning from the city on a bicycle. This man was amazed.

"Agha," he said, "where are you going?"

"To town," my father said.

"But, Agha," said the farmer, "you cannot do this thing. It is eleven miles to town and you look . . . People will laugh at you in such clothes."

"Let them laugh," my father said. "These are my clothes. They fit me."

"Yes, yes, of course they fit you," said the farmer, "but such clothes do not seem right out here, in this dust and heat. Everyone wears overalls out here, Agha."

"Nonsense," said my father. He went on walking.

The farmer followed my father, whom he now regarded as insane.

"At least, at least," he said, "if you insist on wearing those clothes, at least you will not humiliate yourself by *walking* to town. You will at least accept the use of my bicycle."

This farmer was a close friend of my father's family, and he had great respect for my father. He meant well, but my father was dumbfounded. He stared at the man with horror and disgust.

"What?" he shouted. "You ask me to mount one of those crazy contraptions? You ask me to tangle myself in that ungodly piece of junk?" (The Armenian equivalent of junk is a good deal more violent and horrible.) "Man was not made for such absurd inventions," my father said. "Man was not placed on the earth to tangle himself in junk. He was placed here to stand erect and to walk with his feet."

And away he went.

Ah, you can be sure that I worship this man. And now, alone in my room, thinking of these things, tapping out this story, I want to show you that I and my father are the same man.

I shall come soon to the matter of the typewriter, but there is no hurry. I am a story-teller, not an aviator. I am not carrying myself across the Atlantic in the cockpit of an airplane which moves at the rate of two hundred and fifty miles per hour.

It is Monday of this year, 1933, and I am trying to gather as much of eternity into this story as possible. When next this story is read I may be with my father in the earth we both love and I may have sons alive on the surface of this old earth, young fellows whom I shall ask to be humble, as my father has asked me to be humble.

In a moment a century may have elapsed, and I am doing what I can to keep this moment solid and alive.

Musicians have been known to weep at the loss of a musical instrument, or at its injury. To a great violinist his violin is a part of his identity. I am a young man with a dark mind, and a dark way in general, a sullen and serious way. The earth is mine, but not the world. If I am taken away from language, if I am placed in the street, as one more living entity, I become nothing, not even a shadow. I have less honor than the grocer's clerk, less dignity than the doorman at the St. Francis Hotel, less identity than the driver of a taxi-cab.

And for the past six months I have been separated from my writing, and I have been nothing, or I have been walking about unalive, some indistinct shadow in a nightmare of the universe. It is simply that without conscious articulation, without words, without language, I do not exist as myself. I have no meaning, and I might just as well be dead and nameless. It is blasphemous for any living man to live in such a manner. It is an outrage to God. It means that we have got nowhere after all these years.

It is for this reason, now that I have my typewriter again, and have beside me a bundle of clean writing paper, and am sitting in my room, full of tobacco smoke, with my father's photograph watching over me—it is for this reason that I feel as if I have just been resurrected from the dead. I love and worship life, living senses, functioning minds. I love consciousness. I love precision. And life is to be created by every man who has the breath of God within him; and every man is to create his own consciousness, and his own precision, for these things do not exist of themselves. Only confusion and error and ugliness exist of themselves. I have said that I am deeply religious. I am. I believe that I live, and you've got to be religious to believe so miraculous a thing. And I am grateful and I am humble. I do live, so let the years repeat themselves eternally, for I am sitting in my room, stating in words the truth of my being, squeezing the fact from meaninglessness and imprecision. And the living of this moment can never be effaced. It is beyond time.

I despise commerce. I am a young man with no money. There are times when a young man can use a small sum of money to very good advantage, there are times when money to him, because of what it can purchase, is the most important thing of his life. I despise commerce, but I admit that I have some respect for money. It is, after all, pretty important, and it was the lack of it, year after year, that finally killed my father. It wasn't right for a man so poor to wear the sort of clothes he knew he deserved; so my father died. I would like to have enough money to enable me to live simply and to write my life. Years ago, when I labored in behalf of industry and progress and so on, I purchased a small portable typewriter, brand new, for sixty-five dollars. (And what an enormous lot of money that is, if you are poor.) At first this machine was strange to me and I was annoyed by the racket it made when it was in use; late at night this racket was unbearably distressing. It resembled more than anything else silence which has been magnified a thousand times, if such a thing can be. But after a year or two I began to feel a genuine attachment toward the machine, and loved it as a good pianist, who respects music, loves his piano. I never troubled to clean the machine and no matter how persistently I pounded upon it, the machine did not weaken and fall to pieces. I had great respect for it.

And then, in a fit of despondency, I placed this small machine in its case and carried it to the city. I left it in the establishment of a money-lender, and walked through the city with fifteen dollars in my pocket. I was sick of being poor.

I went first to a bootblack and had my shoes polished. When a bootblack is shining my shoes I place him in my place in the chair and I descend and polish his shoes. It is an experience in humility.

Then I went to a theatre. I sat among people to see myself in patterns of Hollywood. I sat and dreamed, looking into the faces of beautiful women. Then I went to a restaurant and sat at a table and ordered all the different kinds of food I ever thought I would like to eat. I ate two dollars' worth of food. The waiter thought I was out of my head, but I told him everything was going along first rate. I tipped the waiter. Then I went out into the city again and began walking along the dark streets, the streets where the women are. I was tired of being poor. I put my typewriter in hock and I began to spend the money. No one, not even the greatest writer, can go on being poor hour after hour, year after year. There is such a thing as saying to hell with art. That's what I said.

After a week I became a little more sober. After a month I got to be very sober and I began to want my typewriter again. I began to want to put words on paper again. To make another beginning. To say something and see if it was the right thing. But I had no money. Day after day I had this longing for my typewriter.

This is the whole story. I don't suppose this is a very artful ending, but it is the ending just the same. The point is this: *day after day I longed for my typewriter.*

This morning I got it back. It is before me now and I am tapping at it, and this is what I have written.

Love, Death, Sacrifice and So Forth

Tom Garner, in the movie, on the screen, a big broad-shouldered man, a builder of railroads, President of the Chicago & Southwestern, staggers, does not walk, into his room, and closes the door.

You know he is going to commit suicide because he has staggered, and it is a movie, and already a long while has passed since the picture began, and something's got to happen real soon, something big, gigantic, as they say in Hollywood, a suicide or a kiss.

You are sitting in the theatre waiting for what you know is going to happen.

Poor Tom has just learned that the male offspring of his second wife is the product of his grown son by his first wife. Tom's first wife committed suicide when she learned that Tom had fallen in love with the young woman who finally became his second wife. This young woman was the daughter of the President of the Santa Clara Railroad. She made Tom fall in love with her so that her father would go on being President of the Santa Clara. Tom had bought the Santa Clara for nine million dollars. Tom's first wife threw herself beneath a streetcar when she found out about Tom's infatuation. She did it by acting, with her face, her eyes and lips and the way she walked. You didn't get to see anything sickening, you saw only the motorman's frantic expression while he tried to bring the car to a stop. You heard and saw the steel wheel grinding, the wheel that killed her. You heard people screaming the way they do about violent things, and you got the idea. The worst had happened. Tom's wife Sally had gone to her Maker.

Sally met Tom when he was a trackwalker and she a teacher in a small country school. Tom confessed to her one day that he did not know how to read, write or do arithmetic. Sally taught Tom to read, write, add, subtract, divide and multiply. One evening after they were married she asked him if he wanted to be a trackwalker all his life, and he said that he did. Sally asked him if he didn't have at least a little ambition, and Tom said he was satisfied, trackwalking was easy work, they had their little home, and Tom got in a lot of fishing on the side. This hurt Sally, and she began to act. Tom saw that it would mean a lot to Sally if he became ambitious. Sitting at the supper table, he said that he would. A strange look came into his eyes, his face acquired great character. You could almost see him forging ahead in life.

Sally sent Tom to school in Chicago, and she did Tom's work as a trackwalker in order to have money with which to pay for his tuition, a great woman, an heroic wife. You saw her one winter night walking along a railroad track, packing tools and oil cans, snow and desolation all around her. It was sad. It was meant to be sad. She was doing it for Tom, so that he would be able to become a great man. The day Tom announced that he had been made foreman of the construction of the Missouri Bridge, Sally announced that she was with child, and Tom said now they could never stop him. With Sally and his baby to inspire him Tom would reach the heights.

Sally gave birth to a son, and while Tom was walking to her bedside you heard symphonic music, and you knew that this was a great moment in Tom's life. You saw Tom enter the dimly lighted room and kneel beside his wife and baby son, and you heard him pray. You heard him say, Our Father which art in heaven, thine the glory and the power, forever and forever. You heard two people in the theatre blowing their noses.

Sally made Tom. She took him from the track and sent him to the president's chair. Then Tom became infatuated with this younger and lovelier woman, and Sally threw herself beneath the streetcar. It was because of what she had done for Tom that her suicide was so touching. It was because of this that tears came to the eyes of so many people in the theatre when Sally destroyed herself.

But Sally's suicide did not have any effect on Tom's infatuation for the younger woman, and after a short while he married the girl, being a practical man part of the time, being practical as long as Hollywood wanted him to be practical. Tom's son, a young man just expelled from college for drunkenness, moved into Tom's house, and had an affair with Tom's second wife.

The result was the baby, a good healthy baby, born of the son instead of the father. Tom's son Tommy is an irresponsible but serious and well-dressed young man, and he really didn't mean to do it. Nature did it. You know how nature is, even in the movies. Tom had been away from home so much, attending to business, and his second wife had been so lonely that she had turned to her husband's son, and he had become her dancing partner.

You saw her holding her hand out to the young irresponsible boy, and you heard her ask him significantly if he would like to dance with her. It took him so long to take her hand that you understood the frightening implication instantly. And she was so maddeningly beautiful, extending her hand to him, that you knew you yourself would never have been able to resist her challenge, even under similar circumstances. There was something irresistible about the perfection of her face and figure, lips so kissable, stance so elegant, body so lovely, soul so needful.

It simply had to happen. Man is flesh, and all that.

So the big railroad builder, the man who always had his way, the man who broke a strike and had forty of his men killed in a riot and a fire, has staggered into his room and closed the door.

And you know the picture is about to end.

The atmosphere of the theatre is becoming electrical with the apprehension of middle-aged ladies who have spent the better parts of their lives in the movies, loving, dying, sacrificing themselves to noble ideals, etc. They've come again to the dark theatre, and a moment of great living is again upon them.

You can feel the spiritual tenseness of all of these ladies, and if you are listening carefully you can actually hear them living fully.

Poor Tom is in there with a terrific problem and a ghastly obligation.

For his honor's sake, for the sake of Hollywood ethics, for the sake of the industry (the third largest in America, I understand), for God's sake, for your sake and my sake, Tom has got to commit suicide. If he doesn't, it will simply mean we have been deceiving ourselves all these years, Shakespeare and the rest of us. We know he'll be man enough to do it, but for an instant we hope he won't, just to see what will happen, just to see if the world we have made will actually smash.

A long while back we made the rules, and now, after all these years, we wonder if they are the genuine ones, or if, maybe, we didn't make a mistake at the outset. We know it's art, and it even looks a little like life, but we know it isn't life, being much too precise.

We would like to know if our greatness must necessarily go on forever being melodramatic.

The camera rests on the bewildered face of Tom's old and faithful secretary, a man who knew Tom as a boy. This is to give you the full implication of Tom's predicament and to create a powerful suspense in your mind.

Then, at a trot, with the same object in view, time hurrying, culminations, ultimates, inevitabilities, Tom's son Tommy comes to the old and faithful secretary and exclaims that he has heard Tom, his father, is ill. He does not know that his father knows. It is a Hollywood moment. You hear appropriate music.

He rushes to the door, to go to his father, this boy who upset the natural order of the universe by having a sexual affair with his father's young wife, and then, bang, the pistol shot.

You know it is all over with the President of the Chicago & Southwestern. His honor is saved. He remains a great man. Once again the industry triumphs. The dignity of life is preserved. Everything is hotsytotsy. It will be possible for Hollywood to go on making pictures for the public for another century.

Everything is precise, for effect. Halt. Symphonic music, Tommy's hand frozen on the door-knob.

The old and faithful secretary knows what has happened, Tommy knows, you know and I know, but there is nothing like seeing. The old and faithful secretary allows the stark reality of the pistol shot to penetrate his old, faithful and orderly mind. Then, since Tommy is too frightened to do so, he forces himself to open the door.

All of us are waiting to see how it happened.

The door opens and we go in, fifty million of us in America and millions more all over the earth.

Poor Tom. He is sinking to his knees, and somehow, even though it is happening swiftly, it seems that this little action, being the last one of a great man, will go on forever, this sinking to the knees. The room is dim, the music eloquent. There is no blood, no disorder. Tom is sinking to his knees, dying nobly. I myself hear two ladies weeping. They know it's a movie, they know it must be fake, still, they are weeping. Tom is man. He is life. It makes them weep to see life sinking to its knees. The movie will be over in a minute and they will get up and go home, and get down to the regular business of their lives, but now, in the pious darkness of the theatre, they are weeping.

All I know is this: that a suicide is not an orderly occurrence with symphonic music. There was a man once who lived in the house next door to my house when I was a boy of nine or ten. One afternoon he committed suicide, but it took him over an hour to do it. He shot himself through the chest, missed his heart, then shot himself through the stomach. I heard both shots. There was an interval of about forty seconds between the shots. I thought afterwards that during the interval he was probably trying to decide if he ought to go on wanting to be dead or if he ought to try to get well.

Then he started to holler. The whole thing was a mess, materially and spiritually, this man hollering, people running, shouting, wanting to do something and not knowing what to do. He hollered so loud half the town heard him.

This is all I know about regular suicides. I haven't seen a woman throw herself under a streetcar, so I can't say about that. This is the only suicide I have any definite information about. The way this man hollered wouldn't please anyone in a movie. It wouldn't make anyone weep with joy.

I think it comes to this: we've got to stop committing suicide in the movies.

1, 2, 3, 4, 5, 6, 7, 8

Walking through Woolworth's in 1927, he saw a small crowd of shoppers working swiftly with their arms over a table stacked high with phonograph records. He went over to find out what it was all about, and it was a special, new Victor and Brunswick records, five cents each, and a wide choice of titles to choose from. Well, he hadn't heard the phonograph in months. He might wind it up again and listen to it. The phonograph was pretty much himself. He had gotten into the machine and come out of it, singing, or being a symphony, or a wild jazz composition. For months he hadn't gone near the phonograph, and it had stood in his room, dusty and mute.

These five-cent records reminded him that he had been silent through the phonograph for a long time, and that he might again enjoy emerging from it.

He selected a half dozen records and took them to his room. He was certain that none of the records could be very good, but he wasn't seeking anything good and he didn't mind how trivial or trite the music might be. If a thing is terribly bad, anything, a man or a piece of music, it is a form of exploration to go through the thing. He knew that he could do this with the worst sort of American jazz. The melody could be idiotic, the orchestration noisy, and so on, but somewhere in the racket he would be able, by listening carefully, to hear the noblest weeping or laughter of mortality. Sometimes it would be a sudden and brief bit of counterpoint, several chords of a banjo perhaps, and occasionally it would be the sadness in the voice of some very poor vocalist singing a chorus of a very insipid song. Something largely accidental, something inevitable.

You could not do this with the finer music. The virtues of the finer music were intentional. They were there for everybody, unmistakably.

It was early August, I think. (I am speaking of myself.) For many months he had not listened to himself through the phonograph, and now he was taking these new records home.

In August a young man is apt to feel unspeakably alive: in those days I was an employee of a telegraph company. I used to sit at a table all day, working a teletype machine, sending and receiving telegrams,

1, 2, 3, 4, 5, 6, 7, 8

and when the day was over I used to feel this unspeakable liveliness, but at the same time I used to feel lost. Absolutely misplaced. I seemed to feel that they had gotten me so deeply into the mechanical idea of the age that I was doomed eventually to become a fragment of a machine myself. It was a way to earn money, this sitting before the machine. I disliked it very much, but it was a way.

He knew that he was lost in it and that they were taking out the insides of him and putting in a complicated mass of wheels and springs and hammers and levers, a piece of junk that worked precisely, doing a specific thing over and over again, precisely.

All day I used to sit at the machine, being a great help to American industry. I used to send important telegrams to important people accurately. The things that were going on had nothing to do with me, but I was sitting there, working for America. What I wanted, I think, was a house. I was living in a cheap rooming house, alone. I had a floor and a roof and a half dozen books. The books I could not read. They were by great writers. I could not read them: I was sitting all day at the table, helping my country to become the most prosperous one in the world. I had a bed. I used to fall asleep sometimes from sheer exhaustion. It would be very late at night or early in the morning. A man cannot sleep anywhere. If a room has no meaning for you, if it is not a part of you, you cannot sleep in it. This room that I was living in was not a part of me. It belonged to anybody who could afford to pay three dollars a week rent for it. I was there, living. I was almost nineteen, crazy as a bat.

He wanted a house, a place in which to return to himself, a space protected by lumber and glass, under the sun, upon the earth.

He took the six records up to his room. Looking out of the small window of his small room, he saw that he was lost. This amused him. It was a thing to make slurring conversation for entertainment. He walked about in his room, his hat still on his head, talking to the place. Well, here we are at home, he said.

I forget what he ate that night, but I know he cooked it on a small gas-range that was provided by the landlady for cooking as well as suicide. He ate something, washed and wiped the dishes he had used, and then turned to the phonograph.

There was a chance for him to find out what it was all about. There was a chance that the information would be hidden in the jazz music. It was a thought. He had learned something about machinery, American machines working, through jazz. He had been able to picture ten thousand humpback New York women in an enormous room, sewing on machines. He had been able to see machines bigger than mountains, machines that did big things, created power, conserved energy, produced flashlights, locomotives, tin cans, saxophones.

It was a small phonograph, not a portable, but a

small Victor. He had had it for years, and he had taken it with him from place to place. It was very impractical to carry such a phonograph around, and he knew it was impractical, but he always carried it with him when he moved from one room to another, or from one city to another. Even if he hadn't used the phonograph for months, he would take it away with him. He liked to feel that it was always there and that whenever he liked he could listen to it. It was like having an enormous sum of money in the bank, a sum so large that you were afraid to touch it. He could listen to any music he liked. He had Roumanian folk songs, Negro spirituals, American westerns, American jazz, Grieg, Beethoven, Gershwin, Zez Confrey, Brahms, Schubert, Irving Berlin, *Where the River Shannon's Flowing, Ave Maria, Vesti La Giubba,* Caruso, Rachmaninoff, Vernon Dalhart, Kreisler, Al Jolson. It was all there, in the records, himself in the music, and for months he had not listened to the phonograph. A silence had come over him and the phonograph, and as time went by, it had become more and more difficult to break the silence.

He had begun to feel lost months ago. One evening, from a moving streetcar, he had suddenly noticed the sky. It was a terrific fact, the existence of the sky. Noticing it, looking up into it, with night coming on, he had realized how lost he had become.

But he hadn't done anything about the matter. He had begun to want a house of his own, but he hadn't done anything to get a house.

He stood over his phonograph, thinking of its

silence and his own silence, the fear in himself to make a noise, to declare his existence.

He lifted the phonograph from the floor and placed it on his small eating table. The phonograph was very dusty, and he spent a leisurely ten minutes cleaning it. When he was through cleaning it, greater fear came over him, and he wanted for a moment to put it back again on the floor and let it remain silent. After a while he wound the machine slowly, hoping secretly that something inside of it would break, so that he would not be able, after all, to make a noise in the world.

I remember clearly how amazed I was when nothing in the machine snapped. I thought, after all these months of silence, how strange. In a moment sound will be emerging from the box. I do not know the scientific name for this sort of fright, but I know that I was very frightened. I felt that it would be best if my being lost were to remain a secret. I felt certain that I no longer wanted to make a noise, and at the same time I felt that, since I had brought home these new records, I ought at least to hear them once before putting them away with the other records I had accumulated.

I listened to the six records, to both sides of them, that night. I had purchased soft needles, so that the phonograph should not make too much of a noise and disturb the other dwellers in the rooming house, but after months of silence, the volume of sound that emerged from the phonograph was very great. It was so great that I had to smoke cigarettes all the time, and I remember the knock at my door.

It was the landlady, Mrs. Liebig. She said, Ah, it is you, Mr. Romano. A little music, is that it? Well . . .

Yes, I said. Several new records. I shall be done with them in a moment.

She hadn't liked the idea of my playing a phonograph in her rooming house, but I had been with her so long, and I had paid so regularly and kept my room so orderly that she hadn't wanted to come right out and tell me so. I knew, however.

The records were all dull and a little boring. All except one. There was one passage of syncopation in this record that was tremendously interesting to me. I played this passage three or four times that night in an effort to understand its significance, but I got nowhere. I understood the passage technically, but I could not determine why it moved me so strangely. It was a bit of counterpoint to a rather romantic and therefore insipid melody. It was eight swift chords on the banjo, repeated fourteen times, while the melody grew in emotional intensity, reached a climax, and then dwindled to silence. *One two three four five six seven eight,* swiftly, fourteen times. The sound was wiry. There was something about the dogged persistence of the passage that got into me, something about it that had always been in me, but never before articulated. I won't mention the name of the composition because I am sure the effect it had on me was largely accidental, largely inevitable for me alone, and that anyone else who might listen to the passage will not be moved by it the way I was moved. The circumstances would have to be pretty much like the circumstances of my own existence at the time, and you would have to be about nineteen years of age, crazy as a bat, etc.

He put away the records and forgot them. Their music joined all the other music he had ever heard and became lost. A week went by. One evening suddenly, in his silence, he heard the passage again, *one two three four five six seven eight,* fourteen times. Another week went by. Every now and then he would hear the passage. It would be when he felt unspeakably alive, when he seemed to possess strength enough to smash everything in the earth that was ugly.

There was nothing for me to do in the city Sundays, so I used to work. Sitting at the teletype machine had become the major business of my life, so I used to work on Sundays too. But on Sundays business would be very slow, and most of the day I would sit around in the office, moping, dreaming, thinking about the house I wanted to get for myself. The teletype machine sends and receives messages. It is a great mechanical triumph, and it put thousands of old time telegraphers out of work. These men used to get as much as a dollar an hour for their work, but when the teletype machine was perfected and put into use these men lost their jobs and young fellows like me who didn't know the first thing about regular telegraphy got their jobs. It was a great stroke of efficiency,

1, 2, 3, 4, 5, 6, 7, 8

the perfection of this machine. It saved the telegraph companies millions of dollars every year. I used to earn about twenty-eight cents an hour, and I used to be able to send and receive twice as many telegrams as the fastest telegraph operator would have been able to receive and send in the same length of time. But on Sundays business would be very slow and the teletype would be silent sometimes for as long as an hour.

One Sunday morning, after a long silence, my machine began to function, so I went over to it to receive and check the message, but it was not a message, not a regular telegram. I read the words, *hello hello hello.* I had never thought of the machine as being related in any way to me. It was there for the messages of other people, and the tapping of this greeting to me seemed very startling. For one thing, it was strictly against company rules to use the machine for anything other than the transmission of regular business. It was a breach of company discipline for a teletype operator, and it was because of this fact that I began to think a great deal of the other operator who had sent me the greeting. I typed the word *hello,* and we began a conversation.

It seemed very strange for me to be using the machine in a way useful to myself. I talked with the other operator for about an hour. It was a girl, and she was working in the operating room at the main office. I was working in one of the numerous branch offices in the city. We did a lot of talking for about an hour, and then suddenly I read the words *wire chief,* so I knew that the big shot had returned to the room and that we would not be able to go on talking.

Suddenly, in the silence, he began to hear the passage again, *one two three four five six seven eight,* over and over again, and it began to have specific meaning for him: the house, the clean earth around it, the warm sun, and another, *one two three four five six seven eight,* himself and this other and the house and the earth and the sun and clear senses and deep sleep and *one two three four five six seven eight,* and meaning and fullness and no sense of being lost and no feeling of being caught.

I began to try to visualize the girl. I began to wonder if she would go out with me to this house I wanted and help me fill it with our lives, together. After a while the teletype machine began to tap again, and again I read *hello hello, wire chief gone.*

It was very splendid, the way it happened, a breach of company discipline and so on.

At five o'clock in the afternoon she came down from the main office and walked into the office where I was working. She hadn't said she was coming down, but the moment she stepped into the office I knew who she was because as soon as I saw her face I began to hear the music, *one two three four five six seven eight,* swiftly, and it was so bad with me that I wanted to leap over the counter and embrace her and tell her about the house.

We talked politely instead.

At six o'clock, when he was through working for

the day, he walked with her out of the city to her house, talking with her, hearing the music over and over again. For the first time in months he began really to laugh. She was splendid. Her mind was deliciously alive; she loved mischief, and in her eyes he seemed to see the earth, the bright earth, full of light and warmth, and the strength of growing things. It was a place to build the house and to be alive and himself.

That evening he played the record over and over again, and finally the landlady came to his room and said, Mr. Romano, it is almost half past eleven.

They got to be pretty good friends, and he began to tell her about the house. At first she didn't really listen to what he said; she merely listened to the way he said it, but after a while she began to listen to everything he had to say, all the insane things about the machines getting into them and destroying them and destroying everything decent in them.

They stopped working Sundays and began going across the bay to Marin County. Every Sunday they walked into the hills of Marin County, talking about the house. All during September and October, 1927, they were together on Sundays, walking in the hills across the bay from San Francisco.

The feeling of being lost began to leave him. There was at least one person in the world who knew that he was alive and attached some importance to the fact, and for a while it looked as if the house he had wanted so long would actually materialize, and he would enter it with this girl, laughing, and they would be in it together, forever and forever.

1, 2, 3, 4, 5, 6, 7, 8

I have said that he was nineteen.

Forever and forever, this is the amusing part. All day long at the teletype machine he would hear the music, *one two three four five six seven eight,* forever and forever and forever, and this girl and this music and the house that was to be, all mingled, and for a while he believed in the inevitability of his hope.

I am coming now to the truth. I am not permitting myself to make a story.

In August and September and October, because of something inexplicable, atmospheric if you like, they were splendidly one, melody and counterpoint, precisely, perfectly, and the dream of eternity was not a fantastic dream.

The house, they wanted. They wanted it desperately. In August and September and October. They wanted themselves desperately. And so on.

Things happen. They happen subtly, quietly, strangely. Everything for a moment is thus: then when one looks again, everything is changed and is now *thus*: a new configuration, the blood thus, the earth thus, and the meaning of life thus. There is nothing you can do about it. Only art is precise and everlastingly itself: everlastingly dependable.

They did not quarrel. The girl did not get sick and die. She did not run off with another young man or with an older rich man.

1, 2, 3, 4, 5, 6, 7, 8

All of a sudden, the melody was silenced, the counterpoint faded away. It was November.

I used to sit in my room, trying to understand what had happened to us. The house. Why, it was laughable. How would I ever be able to own a house on my salary? The feeling of being lost. That was nonsense. It was absolutely stupid. I used to walk up and down my room, smoking one cigarette after another, trying to understand the sudden toppling of the edifice we had built for ourselves. I wanted to know why we no longer wanted to go away from the city. It was not the girl alone. I myself had stopped talking about the house. I myself had stopped hearing the music, and suddenly the silence had returned, and I was standing in the midst of it, again lost, but now without the wish to return to myself. Let it go, I felt. Let it stand as it is. And so on.

During the winter they gradually fell away from one another, and then suddenly in March, 1928, he knew that the whole business was a thing of the past, that it was dead.

Something happened to her. She lost her job. She moved away, to another address, to another city, he didn't know which. He lost track of her.

In June something happened to him.

One afternoon I was sitting at the teletype machine, working it, and all of a sudden I began to hear the passage, *one two three four five six seven eight,* swiftly, and I began to see her face and the landscape

1, 2, 3, 4, 5, 6, 7, 8
that was her eyes, and I began to hear her laughter, *one two three four five six seven eight,* and as I worked the machine this music and the remembrance of this girl and the resurrection of the house we were to have made for ourselves, all these things began to be in my mind the way they had been in the summer, as truth and reality, and I began to feel lost and bewildered and confused.

That evening he played the record, but he listened to it only once because it brought tears to his eyes. He had laughed at the tears, but he had not dared to listen to the music a second time. The whole thing was really very amusing, he thought. He had got the music and the girl and the house together as one significance in his mind, and it was amusing.

But the next day I began trying to locate her. It happened automatically. I was taking a walk and before I knew it I was at her old address, asking the people who had moved into the house if they knew where she had gone. They did not know. I walked until one o'clock in the morning. The music was getting into me again, and I was beginning to hear it very often.

Whenever he sat down to operate the teletype machine, he would begin to hear the music, emerging from the machine, *one two three four five six seven eight.* Every Sunday he found himself begging the machine to bring her to him again. It was preposterous. He knew that she was no longer with the company, and yet he found himself expecting the machine to tap out her old greeting to him, *hello hello hello*. It was preposterous. Absolutely.

He had never known a great deal about her. He had known her name and what she had meant to him, but nothing more.

And the music: over and over again.

One afternoon, he got up from the teletype machine and removed his work jacket. It was a little after two, and he quit his job and went away with his money. I don't want any of the prosperity, he said. He went up to his room and put all the things he wanted to take away with him into two suitcases.

The phonograph and the records he presented to Mrs. Liebig, the landlady. The phonograph is old, he told her, and it is apt to groan now and then, especially when you put on anything by Beethoven. But it still runs. The records aren't much. There is some decent music, but most of the records are monotonous jazz. He was feeling the music while he was speaking to the landlady, and it was really paining him to be leaving the phonograph and the records in a strange house, but he was sure he didn't want them any longer.

Walking from the waiting room of the depot to the train, I could feel the music tearing out my heart, and when the train began to get under way and when the whistle screamed, I was sitting helplessly, weeping for this girl and the house, and sneering at myself for wanting more of life than there was in life to have.

And Man

One morning, when I was fifteen, I got up before daybreak, because all night I hadn't been able to sleep, tossing in bed with the thought of the earth and the strangeness of being alive, suddenly feeling myself a part of it, definitely, solidly. Merely to be standing again, I had thought all night. Merely to be in the light again, standing, breathing, being alive. I left my bed quietly in the darkness of early morning and put on my clothes, a blue cotton shirt, a pair of corduroy pants, stockings and shoes. It was November and it was beginning to turn cold, but I did not wish to put on more clothes. I felt warm enough. I felt almost feverish, and with more clothes

I knew it would not happen. Something was going to happen, and I felt that if I put on too much clothes it would dwindle away and all that I would have would be the remembrance of something expected, then lost.

All through the sleeplessness of the night I could feel turning in me, like a multitude of small and large wheels, some swift and wordless thought, on the verge of articulation, some vast remembrance out of time, a fresh fullness, a new solidity, a more graceful rhythm of motion emerging from the hurried growth that had taken place in me during the summer.

With the beginning of spring that year came the faint and fragmentary beginning of this thought, burning in my mind with the sound of fire eating substance, sweeping through my blood with the impatience and impetuosity of a deluge. Before the beginning of this thought I had been nothing more than a small and sullen boy, moving through the moments of my life with anger and fear and bitterness and doubt, wanting desperately to know the meaning and never quite being able to do so. But now in November I was as large physically as a man, larger, for that matter, than most men. It was as if I had leaped suddenly from the form of myself as a boy to the vaster form of myself as a man, and to the vaster meaning of myself as something specific and alive. Look at him, my relatives were saying, every part of his body is growing, especially his nose. And they made sly jokes about my private organs, driving me out of my head with shame. How about it? they asked, even the ladies. Is it growing? Do you dream of big women, hundreds of them?

I don't know what you're talking about, I used to say. But I did know. Only I was ashamed. Look at that nose, they used to say. Just look at that enormous nose on his face.

During the summer I sometimes stopped suddenly before a mirror to look at myself, and after a moment I would turn away, feeling disgusted with my ugliness, worrying about it. I couldn't understand how it was that I looked utterly unlike what I imagined myself to be. In my mind I had another face, a finer, a more subtle and dignified expression, but in the mirror I could see the real reflection of myself, and I could see that it was ugly, thick, bony, and coarse. I thought it was something finer, I used to say to myself. I hadn't bothered before about looking at myself. I had thought that I knew precisely how I looked, and the truth distressed me, making me ashamed. Afterwards I stopped caring. I am ugly, I said. I know I am ugly. But it is only my face.

And I could believe that my face was not the whole of it. It was simply a part of myself that was growing with the rest, an outward part, and therefore not as important as the inward part. The real growth was going on inside, not simply within the boundaries of my physical form, but outward through the mind and through the imagination to the real largeness of being, the limitless largeness of consciousness, of knowing and feeling and remembering.

I began to forget the ugliness of my face, turning again to the simplicity and kindliness of the face I believed to be my own, the face of myself in the secrecy of my heart, in the night light of sleep, in the truth of thought.

It is true that my face seems ugly, I said, but it is also true that it is not ugly. I know it is not, because I have seen it with my own eyes and shaped it with my own thought, and my vision has been clear and my thought has been clean. It cannot be ugly.

But how was anyone to understand the real truth, how was anyone to see the face that I saw, and know that it was the real reflection of my being? This worried me a lot. There was a girl in my class at high school whom I worshipped, and I wanted this girl to see that my face, the face she saw, was not the truthful one, that it was merely a part of the growth that was going on. And I wanted her to be able to see with me the truthful face, because I felt that if she did see it, she would understand my love for her, and she would love me.

All through the night I had tossed with the thought of myself somehow alive on the earth, somehow specific and at the same time a substance that was changing and would always change, from moment to moment, imperceptibly, myself entering one moment thus, and emerging thus, over and over again. I wanted to know what it was in me that was static and permanent and endurable, what it was that belonged not to myself alone but to the body of man, to his legend, to the truth of his motion over the earth, moment after moment, century after century. All through the night it seemed that I would soon learn, and in the morning I left my bed, standing in the darkness and the stillness, feeling the splendor of having form and weight and motion, having, I hoped, meaning.

I walked quietly through the darkness of the house and emerged, standing for a moment in the street, acknowledging the magnificence of our earth, the large beauty of limitless space about our insignificant forms, the remoteness of the great celestial bodies of our universe, our oceans, our mountains, our valleys, the great cities we had made, the strong and clean and fearless things we had done. The small boats we had made and sent over the wild waters, the slow growth of railroads, the slow accumulation of knowledge, the slow but everlasting seeking after God, in the vastness of the universe, in the solidity of our own earth, in the glory of our own small beings, the simplicity of our own hearts.

Merely to be standing, merely to be breathing that day was a truth in the nature of an inexplicable miracle. After all these years, I thought . . . I myself standing here in the darkness, breathing, knowing that I live. I wanted to say something in language, with the words I had been taught in school, something solemn and dignified and joyous . . . to express the gratitude I felt to God. But it was impossible. There were no words with which to say it. I could feel the magnificence coming through the cold clean air, touching my blood, racing through it, dancing, but there were no words with which to say it.

There was a fire hydrant in our street, and I had always wanted to hurdle it, but I had always been afraid to try. It was made of metal and I was made of flesh and blood and bone, and if I did not clear the fire hydrant, leaping swiftly, my flesh would smash against it, paining me, perhaps breaking a bone in one of my legs.

Suddenly I was leaping over the hydrant, and, clearing it, I was thinking, I can do it now. I can do anything now.

I hurdled the fire hydrant six or seven times, leaping away over it, hearing myself landing solidly on the earth, feeling tremendous.

Then I began to walk, not slowly, not casually, but vigorously, leaping now and then because I couldn't help it. Each time I came to a tree, I leaped and caught a limb, making it bend with my weight, pulling myself up and letting myself down. I walked into the town, into the streets where we had put up our buildings, and suddenly I saw them for this first time, suddenly I was really *seeing* them, and they were splendid. The city was almost deserted, and I seemed to be alone in it, seeing it as it really was, in all its fineness, with all its meaning, giving it its real truth, like the truth of my hidden face, the inward splendor. The winter sun came up while I walked and its light fell over the city, making a cool warmth. I touched the buildings, feeling them with the palms of my hands, feeling the meaning of the solidity and the precision. I touched the plate-glass windows, the brick, the wood and the cement.

When I got home, everyone was awake, at the breakfast table. Where have you been? they asked. Why did you get up so early?

AND MAN

I sat in my chair at the table, feeling great hunger. Shall I tell them? I thought. Shall I try to tell them what is happening? Will they understand? Or will they laugh at me?

Suddenly I knew that I was a stranger among them, my own people, and I knew that while I loved them, I could not go out to them, revealing the truth of my being. Each of us is alone, I thought. Each is a stranger to the other. My mother thinks of me as a pain she once suffered, a babe at her breast, a small child in the house, a boy walking to school, and now a young man with an ugly face, a restless and half-mad fellow who moves about strangely.

We ate mush in those days. It was cheap and we were poor, and the mush filled a lot of space. We used to buy it in bulk, by the pound, and we had it for breakfast every morning. There was a big bowl of it before me, about a pound and a half of it, steaming, and I began to swallow the food, feeling it sinking to my hunger, entering my blood, becoming myself and the change that was going on in me.

No, I thought. I cannot tell them. I cannot tell anyone. Everyone must see for himself. Everyone must seek the truth for himself. It is here, and each man must seek it for himself. But the girl, I thought. I should be able to tell her. She was of me. I had taken her name, her form, the outward one and the inward one, and I had breathed her into me, joining her meaning to my meaning, and she was of my thought, of my motion in walking over the earth, and of my sleep. I would tell her. After I had revealed my hidden face to her, I would speak to the girl about ourselves, about our being alive together, on the same earth, in the same moment of eternity. I had never spoken to the girl. I had loved her secretly, worshipping her, worshipping the very things she touched, her books, her desk, the earth over which she moved, the air about her, but I had never had the courage to speak to her. I wanted my speaking to mean so much, to be so important to each of us, that I was afraid even to think of breaking the silence between us.

I went for a little walk, I replied.

Everyone began to laugh at me, even my mother. What's the matter with you? they asked. Why can't you sleep? Are you in love again? Is that it? Are you dreaming of some girl?

I sat at the table, swallowing the hot food, hearing them laughing at me. I cannot tell them, I thought. They are laughing at me. They think it is something to laugh about. They think it is a little joke.

I began to blush, thinking of the girl and worrying about something to say that would satisfy and silence them, stopping their laughter. Then they began to laugh louder than ever, and I couldn't help it, I began to laugh too.

Yes, they laughed. It must be some girl. Look how handsome he is getting to be. Dreaming about a girl always does that.

I ate all the mush in the bowl and got up from the table. If I try to tell them the truth, I thought, they will laugh more than ever.

I'm going to school, I said, and I left the house. But I knew that I would not go to school that day. I had decided not to go in the middle of the night, when I had been unable to sleep. In school, in that atmosphere, it would never happen. I would never be able to understand what it was that turned in me, circling toward truth, and it would be lost, maybe forever. I decided to walk into the country, and be alone with the thought, helping it to emerge from the bewilderment and confusion of my mind, and the fever of my blood, carrying it to silence and simplicity, giving it a chance to reach its fullness and be whole.

Walking through the country, moving quietly among the leafless grape vines and fig trees, the thought became whole, and I knew the truth about myself and man and the earth and God.

At the proper hour I returned home, as if I were coming home from school, and the following day I went to school. I knew I would be asked for an excuse and an explanation for my absence, and I knew that I would not lie about it. I could tell them that I had been at home, sick with a cold, but I didn't want to do it. There would be a punishment, but I didn't care about that. Let them punish me if they liked. Let old man Brunton give me a strapping. I had walked into the country, into the silence, and I had found the truth. It was more than anything they would ever be able to teach. It was something that wasn't in any of their books. Let them punish me. I wanted also to impress the girl. I wanted her to understand that I had strength, that I could tell the truth and be punished for it, that I would not make up a cheap lie just to get out of a strapping. My telling the truth ought to mean something to her, I thought. Being so much a part of myself, she would be able to see beneath the surface and understand what I had done, and why.

After the roll was taken, my name was called and our teacher said: You were not at school yesterday. Have you brought an excuse?

No, I said, I have not.

Suddenly I felt myself to be the object of the laughter of everyone in the class-room, and I could imagine everyone thinking: What a stupid fellow! I looked at this girl whom I loved so much and I saw that she too was laughing, but I would not believe it. This sometimes happens. It happens when a man has given another person his own dignity and meaning, and the other person has not acquired that dignity and meaning. I saw and heard the girl laughing at me, but I would not believe it. I hadn't intended to entertain her. I hadn't intended to entertain anyone, and the laughter made me angry.

Why were you away from school? said the teacher. Where were you?

I was in the country, I said, walking.

Now the laughter was greater than ever, and I saw the girl I secretly loved laughing with the others, as if I meant nothing to her, as if I hadn't made her a part of myself. I began to feel ill and defiant, and there was warm perspiration on the palms of my hands.

The teacher stood over me, trembling. One must, perhaps, be a teacher to be able to appreciate precisely how angry she felt. For years she had been asking boys why they had been absent from school, and for years the boys had replied that they had been at home, ill. She had known that in most cases they had not told the truth, but the tradition had been maintained and everything had remained solid in her world. Now everything was being shattered, and she was standing over me, trembling with rage. I think she tried to shake me, and I would not let her do it, holding myself solidly. For a moment she budged at me, hating me, and then she said, You Armenians, you, you . . . and I thought she would burst into tears. I felt sorry for her, for the stupidity she had preserved in herself after so many years of trying to teach school, a woman almost fifty years of age.

And I hadn't meant to hurt her. That hadn't been my object at all. I had meant simply to tell the truth. I had meant to reveal to the girl my true face, the face which had been shaped by the dignity and simplicity of man and which she had helped to shape, and I had meant to reveal to her the truth of my presence on earth. And then her laughter, just like the laughter of the others . . . it mangled something in me, and I stood in the midst of the noise, embarrassed and bewildered, bleeding, and breaking to pieces. God damn it, I thought. This is not true. God damn it, this is a lie.

But I knew that I was deceiving myself. And I knew that I would never be able to speak to the girl about my love for her, and the meaning of that love to me, and to the earth and the universe, and to man.

I was sent to the principal of the school, and he stood over me, grumbling in a deep voice. You, he said, you are a disgrace to this school. You are a disgrace to your own race. You break rules. Then you come to school flaunting your crime. What have you to say for yourself.

Nothing, I said.

Why did you do it? he asked.

I wanted to walk, I said.

You could have waited till Saturday, he said.

No, I said. I had to walk yesterday.

Can you think of any reason why I shouldn't strap you? he asked.

That's up to you, I said.

I was angry. I felt bitter about the girl, and I wasn't afraid of the principal, or of the strapping I knew he would give me. It was all over. I would have to walk alone with the secret. I would have to accept the sickness in me that the girl had made by laughing, but the truth would remain whole and I would have it to keep forever, walking alone, in the secrecy of my heart.

The strapping made me cry, big as I was, strong as I was. While I cried, though, I knew that it wasn't the strapping that was hurting me . . . it was this other thing, this incredible blindness everywhere. I cried bitterly, and when I returned to class my eyes were red and I was ashamed, and the whole class was laughing at me, even the girl.

After school, walking alone, I tried to heal the wound in my heart, and I began to think again of the swift and bright truth of being, the truth I had earned for myself by walking alone through the silence of the earth, and walking, thinking of it, I could feel myself becoming whole again, and I could hear myself laughing through the vastness of the secret space I had discovered.

The truth was the secret, God first, the word, the word God, out of all things and beyond, spaceless and timeless, then the void, the silent emptiness, vaster than any mortal mind could conceive, abstract and precise and real and lost, the substance in the emptiness, again precise and with weight and solidity and form, fire and fluid, and then, walking through the vineyards, I had seen it thus, the whole universe, quietly there in the mind of man, motionless and dark and lost, waiting for man, for the thought of man, and I felt the stirring of inanimate substance in the earth, and in myself like the swift growth of the summer, life emerging from time, the germ of man springing from the rock and the fire and the fluid to the face of man, and to the form, to the motion and the thought, suddenly in the emptiness, the thought of man, stirring there. And I was man, and this was the truth I had brought out of the emptiness, walking alone through the vineyards.

I had seen the universe, quietly in the emptiness, secret, and I had revealed it to itself, giving it meaning and grace and the truth that could come only from the thought and energy of man, and the truth was man, myself, moment after moment, and man, century after century, and man, and the face of God in man, and the sound of the laughter of man in the vastness of the secret, and the sound of his weeping in the darkness of it, and the truth was myself and I was man.

A
Curved Line

I was living next door to the high school. In the evenings the lights would go on and I would see men and women in the rooms. I would see them moving about but I wouldn't be able to hear them. I could see that they were saying something among themselves and I thought I would like to go among them and listen. It was a place to go. I didn't want to improve my mind. I was through with all that. I was getting a letter from the Pelman Institute of America every two weeks. I wasn't taking their course. I wasn't even opening the envelopes. I knew exactly what they were saying. They were saying Chesterton and Ben Lindsay had taken their course and now had fine big brains, especially Chesterton. I knew they were telling me I too could have a fine big brain, but I wasn't opening the envelopes. I was turning the matter over to my niece who was four years old. I was thinking maybe she would like to take the course and have a brain like the wise men of the world. I was giving the letters to my niece, and she was taking them and sitting on the floor and cutting them with a pair of scissors. It was a fine thing. The Institute is a great American idea. My niece is cutting the letters with a small pair of scissors.

It was a place to go at night. I was tired of the radio. I had heard NRA speeches, excerpts from Carmen, Tosti's "Goodbye" and "Trees" every night for over a year. Sometimes twice a night. I knew what would happen every night. It was the same downtown. I knew all the movies, what to expect. The pattern never changed. It was the same with symphonies even. Once a lady conducted, but it was the same. Beethoven's Fifth, "The Sorcerer's Apprentice" and "The Blue Danube Waltz." It's been going on for years and years. The thing that worries me is that my great-grandchildren are going to have to listen to "The Blue Danube Waltz" too. It's gotten so that even when the music isn't being played, we hear it. It's gotten into us. Years ago I used to like these fine things, but lately the more pathetic things interest me.

I thought I would go among the people at the night school and listen to them. Going to the school was like walking from one room into another, it was so close. I liked the idea of walking headlong into a group of people who were either very lonely or pathetically ambitious.

The night I went was a Tuesday. The classes were English for Foreigners, Sewing, Dressmaking and Millinery, Leather Work, Wood Work, Radio, Arithmetic, Navigation, Theory of Flight, Typewriting and Commercial Art. I had the printed schedule.

I went to the class in Commercial Art. Beauty with a motive. Practical grace. I didn't know what to expect, but I walked in and sat down. There was a fat woman who gasped when she talked, and always talked. She was the teacher, and she had memorized a number of things from books about art and when I was in hearing distance I heard her gasp, "There are five arts, painting, sculpture, architecture, music, and poetry." She was telling this to a middle-aged, dried-up little lady who was amazed, almost astounded. The little lady had just come to class, and she hadn't heard. It was news to her, and she was amazed that there were five arts. It appeared as if she believed one might have been sufficient. There was a sheet of white paper on the table before her, pencil, bottle of ink and pen. She was delighted with the whole idea. She began to draw a picture of Marlene Dietrich. She had a ten-cent movie magazine to copy from, but her sketch didn't look like Marlene Dietrich. Everything was out of proportion. It looked like a very good Matisse. Only a very shrewd art critic would have been able to tell that it was not an original Matisse. It had all the artless subtlety. It was certainly the face of a woman. The dried-up lady couldn't think of anything else to draw. There were three other women drawing pictures of Marlene Dietrich. It was part of the course.

The men were painting display cards. They were thinking of increasing their incomes.

I heard the women talking about inspiration, and one of the younger women actually looked inspired, but I suppose she was slightly ill.

One of the men was making a pen and ink sketch of Lincoln. He was *absolutely* inspired. The instant I saw him I could tell he was aflame with wonderful sentiments. Every student of art draws Lincoln. There is something about the man. If you start to draw him, no matter how poorly you draw it will look exactly like Lincoln. It's the spirit, the inspiration. No one remembers how he looked. His face is like a trademark. The man had worked his sketch to the point where it was all but finished, and he was amazed. He was a man in his late thirties, and he wore a small Hitler-style moustache. I have reason to believe, however, that he was not a Nazi. It is simply that people, unknown to one another and separated by oceans and continents, are apt, now and then, to come upon the same sort of revelation in regard to some great human problem, such as sex, or to grow the same style of moustache. There is the well-known case of Havelock Ellis and D. H. Lawrence, beards and all. I sat at the table behind the man with the Nazi moustache. The teacher had said that she would be with me in a moment. I sat and watched the man who was sketching Lincoln. He was looking about nervously to see if anyone was noticing what he had done. He expected something to happen. He hadn't known he had had it in him. The others were mere sign painters.

There was a young girl on the opposite side of his table. She was doing a charcoal portrait of a pretty girl. I thought it was someone she knew. It was Clara Bow. I hadn't noticed the movie magazine she was copying from. She had already made her sketch of Marlene Dietrich. All over the class it was this way.

The man who was sketching Lincoln wanted the girl to notice what he had done, but she was busy putting the finishing touches on Clara Bow. Finally, with the will and impetuosity of the true artist, he got up and walked past the girl to get to the pencil sharpener. He wasn't using his pencil. He was making a pen and ink sketch of Lincoln. On his way back to his seat, he stood over the girl, studying carefully her sketch of Clara Bow. The girl couldn't draw with the man looking over her shoulder. She couldn't move her hand. She was embarrassed. The man said her sketch was very good, but that she hadn't shaded the eyes just right. Having made a sketch of Lincoln, he had become a graduate art critic. He wanted to talk about art first. The girl didn't know what to say. She said something I didn't quite hear. It was something apologetic and not well articulated. I felt sorry for the man. His idea hadn't worked. He had expected something to happen. He had expected a warm interest in him from the girl. He had hoped she would ask to see what he had done, and then he would have thrilled her with his sketch of Lincoln. It hadn't worked. He sat down sullenly and began to put the last touches to Lincoln. Then he signed his name to the work and ran a heavy line beneath his name, giving it force and character. When the roll was taken I found out that the girl's name was Harriet. I didn't get the last name. She looked to be a clerk in the basement of some big department store. She was probably lonely too.

Now the teacher was free to introduce me to art. She stood over me and gasped, and I got a strong odor from her. She began with the five arts and kept on. She had a schedule. She enjoyed going through the schedule, or else it was simply that, like so many teachers, she was unmarried and had to do something, had to talk at least. The first thing I began listening to was about line. It took me that long to get used to her odor.

"By line," she gasped, "we mean the boundaries of shapes. A vertical line denotes activity and growth. A horizontal line denotes rest and repose." She had it pat. "A straight line is masculine," she said. "A curved line is feminine." She went on gasping. I couldn't tell what pleasure she got from it. I certainly hadn't encouraged her. "A vertical line," she said, "slightly curved is considered a line of beauty." There was an exclamation mark in her voice.

"Considered?" I said. "How do you mean?"

Then she understood that I was a radical, and that I was out for no good. She became confused for a moment, then blushed with bitterness, then walked away to get me paper and a pencil. She placed the paper and pencil before me and told me I could draw anything I liked. I tried to draw the dried-up lady who had been amazed about art, and while I was doing so I could hear the teacher gasping to someone else, "There are three fundamental forms. They are the sphere, the cone, the cylinder, or modifications of them." My sketch of the amazed lady was very poor. I hadn't been able to get her amazement into it.

After an hour there was a short recess. Everyone sighed and went into the hall or out on the school steps. I offered the man who had sketched Lincoln a cigarette. He didn't smoke, but he got to talking. He talked in a low dreary voice. We stood on the school steps and I listened to him while I smoked a cigarette. It was February. The evening was mild. I was standing there smoking, listening to the man. I didn't get a word of what he was saying. I told him his sketch of Lincoln was as good as the one he had copied it from, maybe better. When the bell rang we walked back to the room and sat down again.

The genius of the class came at eight for the second period only. She was a woman of about forty with a well-rounded body and gold teeth in her mouth. She wore a green sweater tight, and she was the only artist in the class who worked standing. She stood at the front of the class with her legs apart, one of those forty-year-old women who have young bodies. She was sketching a small plaster reproduction of a nude Grecian youth. With her back to me I could admire her, and there are women who are lovely from this point of view and unbearable from any other. One could sit and look at her for a long while, thinking about lines and which were feminine and which masculine, which denoted activity and which repose. It was a thing to do, a way to kill time. She had an old face, but from where I sat I couldn't see her face.

It felt splendid to be among such a group of people,

and walking home after class I decided I would go back the next evening and find out more about the man who had sketched Lincoln, and the girl he secretly loved, and the lady in the green sweater, and the amazed one, and the fat teacher who gasped. It would be something to do for a while, a place to go in the evening.

Snake

Walking through the park in May, he saw a small brown snake slipping away from him through grass and leaves, and he went after it with a long twig, feeling as he did so the instinctive fear of man for reptiles.

Ah, he thought, our symbol of evil, and he touched the snake with the twig, making it squirm. The snake lifted its head and struck at the twig, then shot away through the grass, hurrying fearfully, and he went after it.

It was very beautiful, and it was amazingly clever, but he intended to stay with it for a while and find out something about it.

The little brown snake led him deep into the park, so that he was hidden from view and alone with it. He had a guilty feeling that in pursuing the snake he was violating some rule of the park, and he prepared a remark for anyone who might discover him. I am a student of contemporary morality, he thought he would say, or, I am a sculptor and I am studying the structure of reptiles. At any rate, he would make some sort of reasonable explanation.

He would not say that he intended to kill the snake.

He moved beside the frightened reptile, leaping now and then to keep up with it, until the snake became exhausted and could not go on. Then he squatted on his heels to have a closer view of it, holding the snake before him by touching it with the twig. He admitted to himself that he was afraid to touch it with his hands. To touch a snake was to touch something secret in the mind of man, something one ought never to bring out into the light. That sleek gliding, and that awful silence, *was* once man, and now that man had come to this last form, here were snakes still moving over the earth as if no change had ever taken place.

The first male and female, biblical; and evolution. Adam and Eve, and the human embryo.

It was a lovely snake, clean and graceful and precise. The snake's fear frightened him and he became panic stricken thinking that perhaps all the snakes in the park would come quietly to the rescue of the little brown snake, and surround him with their malicious silence and the unbearable horror of their evil forms. It was a large park and there must be thousands of snakes in it. If all the snakes were to find out that he was with this little snake, they would easily be able to paralyze him.

He stood up and looked around. All was quiet. The silence was almost the biblical silence of *in the beginning*. He could hear a bird hopping from twig to twig in a low earthbush near by, but he was alone with the snake. He forgot that he was in a public park, in a large city. An airplane passed overhead, but he did not see or hear it. The silence was too emphatic and his vision was too emphatically focused on the snake before him.

In the garden with the snake, unnaked, in the beginning, in the year 1931.

He squatted on his heels again and began to commune with the snake. It made him laugh, inwardly and outwardly, to have the form of the snake so substantially before him, apart from his own being, flat on the surface of the earth instead of subtly a part of his own identity. It was really a tremendous thing. At first he was afraid to speak aloud, but as time went on he became less timid, and he began to speak in English to it. It was very pleasant to speak to the snake.

All right, he said, here I am, after all these years, a young man living on the same earth, under the same sun, having the same passions. And here you are before me, the same. The situation is the same. What do you intend to do? Escape? I will not let you escape. What have you in mind? How will you defend yourself? I intend to destroy you. As an obligation to man.

The snake twitched before him helplessly, unable to avoid the twig. It struck at the twig several times and then became too tired to bother with it. He drew away the twig, and heard the snake say, Thank you.

He began to whistle to the snake, to see if the music would have any effect on its movements, if it would make the snake dance. You are my only love, he whistled; Schubert made into a New York musical comedy; *my only love, my only love;* but the snake would not dance. Something Italian perhaps, he thought, and began to sing *la donna e mobile,* intentionally mispronouncing the words in order to amuse himself. He tried a Brahms lullaby, but the music had no effect on the snake. It was tired. It was frightened. It wanted to get away.

He was amazed at himself suddenly; it had occurred to him to let the snake flee, to let it glide away and be lost in the lowly worlds of its kind. Why should he allow it to escape?

He lifted a heavy boulder from the ground and thought: Now I shall bash your head with this rock and see you die.

To destroy that evil grace, to mangle that sinful loveliness.

But it was very strange. He could not let the rock fall on the snake's head, and he began suddenly to feel very sorry for it. I am sorry, he said, dropping the boulder. I beg your pardon. I see now that I have only love for you.

And he wanted to touch the snake with his hands, to hold it and understand the truth of its touch. But it was difficult. The snake was frightened and each time he extended his hands to touch it, the snake turned on him and charged. I have only love for you, he said. Do not be afraid. I am not going to hurt you.

Then, swiftly, he lifted the snake from the earth, learned the true feel of it, and dropped it. There, he said. Now I know the truth. A snake is cold, but it is clean. It is not slimy, as I thought.

He smiled upon the little brown snake. You may go now, he said. The inquisition is over. You are yet alive. You have been in the presence of man, and you are yet alive. You may go now.

But the snake would not go away. It was exhausted with fear.

He felt deeply ashamed of what he had done, and angry with himself. Jesus, he thought, I have scared the little snake. It will never get over this. It will always remember me squatting over it.

For God's sake, he said to the snake, go away. Return to your kind. Tell them what you saw, you yourself, with your own eyes. Tell them what you felt. The sickly heat of the hand of man. Tell them of the presence you felt.

Suddenly the snake turned from him and spilled itself forward, away from him. Thank you, he said. And it made him laugh with joy to see the little snake throwing itself into the grass and leaves, thrusting itself away from man. Splendid, he said; hurry to them and say that you were in the presence of man and that you were not killed. Think of all the snakes that live and die without ever meeting man. Think of the distinction it will mean for you.

It seemed to him that the little snake's movements away from him were the essence of joyous laughter, and he felt greatly pleased. He found his way back to the path, and continued his walk.

In the evening, while she sat at the piano, playing softly, he said: A funny thing happened.

She went on playing. A funny thing? she asked.

Yes, he said. I was walking through the park and I saw a little brown snake.

She stopped playing and turned on the bench to look at him. A snake? she said. How ugly!

No, he said. It was beautiful.

What about it?

Oh, nothing, he said. I just caught it and wouldn't let it go for a while.

But why?

For no good reason at all, he said.

She walked across the room and sat beside him, looking at him strangely.

Tell me about the snake, she said.

It was lovely, he said. Not ugly at all. When I touched it, I felt its cleanliness.

I am so glad, she said. What else?

I wanted to kill the snake, he said. But I couldn't. It was too lovely.

I'm so glad, she said. But tell me everything.

That's all, he said.

But it isn't, she said. I know it isn't. Tell me everything.

It is very funny, he said. I was going to kill the snake, and not come here again.

Aren't you ashamed of yourself? she said.

Of course I am, he said.

What else? she said. What did you think, of me, when you had the snake before you?

You will be angry, he said.

Oh, nonsense. It is impossible for me to be angry with you. Tell me.

Well, he said, I thought you were lovely but evil.

Evil?

I told you you would be angry.

And then?

Then I touched the snake, he said. It wasn't easy, but I picked it up with my hands. What do you make of this? You've read a lot of books about such things. What does it mean, my picking up the snake?

She began to laugh softly, intelligently. Why, she laughed, it means, it simply means that you are an idiot. Why, it's splendid.

Is that according to Freud? he said.

Yes, she laughed. According to Freud.

Well, anyway, he said, it was very fine to let the snake go free.

Have you ever told me you loved me? she asked.

You ought to know, he said. I do not remember one or two things I have said to you.

No, she said. You have never told me.

She began to laugh again, feeling suddenly very happy about him. You have always talked of other things, she said. Irrelevant things. At the most amazing times. She laughed.

This snake, he said, was a little brown snake.

And that explains it, she said. You have never intruded.

What the hell are you talking about? he said.

I'm so glad you didn't kill the snake, she said.

She returned to the piano, and placed her hands softly upon the keys.

I whistled a few songs to the snake, he said. I whistled a fragment from Schubert's Unfinished Symphony. I would like to hear that. You know, the melody that was used in a musical comedy called *Blossom Time*. The part that goes, *you are my only love, my only love,* and so on.

She began to play softly, feeling his eyes on her hair, on her hands, her neck, her back, her arms, feeling him studying her as he had studied the snake.

Big Valley Vineyard

Jew Strawinsky, the nose and mouth in the aquarium, swimming, and Russian Diaghilev, seated with legs crossed, sending the girls up on their dancing toes. The leaves of all the vines in the valley were drying, for the fruit was gone, the red and the purple; the farmers sat and talked.

Tender Cocteau, a dandy to the last, more nervously alive than alive, a boy with long fingers and a pallor. And Satie, bearded like a pawnshop ghost gone broke.

French music, silent during the war, awoke with something of a start the day after the armistice, as who did not, music or man? We lived, as it were, alertly asleep before, but then, after that day, we lived alertly, but awake. Refer to the advertisements about automobiles. There is a place to go for every man. Debussy (the man himself) was dead, Ravel was ill and frightened, and everywhere it was dawn and at dawn man knows a sickness not known at night or during the day.

Out in the vineyards we labored with the vines, speaking fraternally with peons from Mexico, admiring Villa the bandit and Orozco the maniac with the brushes and the paint.

First of all, it was argued (by whom it does not matter) that impressionism was dead. This meant, if anything, that impressionism was *also* dead, along with the soldiers and along with the half dozen decent ideas about civilization. It was said we no longer had any. It was determined (somewhere, in some philosopher's brain) that because we were soft, it did not necessarily follow that we were civilized. There was some discussion of the importance of softness, whether or not it meant what it was hoped it meant.

Barbarians were needed. Real barbarians, things to have life explosively, the war having been waged with undue politeness, particularly in the newspapers and afterwards in the memoirs of generals. And still afterwards in the class-room history books. No victory, all nations having lost their men, the bishop still being pious and a liar, and even though the queen was vilely raped, the king quietly persisted in declaring himself potent. The truth. The truth.

It shall be known. Facts shall be substituted.

As for Teutonic robustness, rubbish. For robustness of any kind, of any race. Such men as are, are alone in selves and amid mobs in race. In Russia: well, God and Trotzky were exiled. Flower and seed and tremble and tumble and the mouths of all the dead, the eloquence of all the silenced mouths.

As for the economic and political upheavals (you are invited to examine the terms) reverberating deeply through the bowels of the several continents, scattering rodents, reptiles and insects, it would be sheer folly to speak seriously of anything in this connection, other than, perhaps, the moustache of Mr. Morgan and the state of his digestion. It is, indeed, a very delicate and complex relation, since not once did any of his associates declare for a renaissance of capitalistic art and hatred for the proletariat. They sat quietly consuming the public, men, women, and children. It is not sad, not so very sad. They themselves had their children kidnapped by the monster they created in the mind of man. There was a gradual return to the laws of fairy tales.

The melodic vein of virtuosi cannot be compared to the steady ripening of fruit, and when the pruning of a vine is at hand, only the dullest of farmers remains unmoved by the aesthetic impulse to dance westward to the sun which brings forth the shape of peach and pear and grape.

And least of all could the peons refrain from singing while they worked.

The monumental forms, so aptly titled by the towering men of books, grew first in plants anonymously, belonging to man, tutored or unlearned, and afterwards were plagiarized by small suns whose light was dim, whose fruit was horrible with rot. With sonority alone it is futile to be content, since a dry hole in the continent does not make a lake, or a torrent of rain without a path, a river.

Lord Berners at the piano, sipping a cocktail, while Leonidine Massine, sweet with sadness, glows angularly in ballet poses at the faces lost in the crowd.

In Venice there were festivals.

For two years I had the honor of spending most of my life in the great fiction room of the public library, and it was there that I remembered the vines. I was asked not to read Zola, and I replied to the old lady who doubtlessly loved me as she would have loved a son had she had one, I thank you piously; I intend only to have the book on my table, for the presence; I seldom read words at all; I run my fingers over the pages for the texture; thus I have held Balzac in my hand and touched the cheek of Madame Sand.

Living in the fiction room of the public library, I recalled that the vines stood in their places in the great warm valley of my awakening, and that although I might never return to tend them, they would stand beneath the sun forever, calmly bearing the ecstasy of producing leaf and fruit, calmly a part of my earth and my life and my death, calmly mothering my ghosts. I spoke casually of this to strangers I met in the fiction room, and we agreed that while the agricultural life could never be economically justified (on account of taxes, frost, lack of rain, new children, leaks in the roof, monopolies and intimidation), it could never be dismissed as unethical or improper, as the practice of law is unethical, and the passing of judgment in courts improper, indecent and vile.

Meanwhile, it was very lively in parts of the country, and I myself, walking to the sanctuary of my room, heard one evening the tender love call of the male cat for the female. And I knew it was not lust that herded me, as cattle are herded, to the bed of the lonely harlot whose sad room overlooked the alley between Mariposa and Tulare Streets. Nevertheless, it was not without tenderness that I was sent through the darkness of the hall to the earth on the floor below, and my own life, and often it was with virtue and truth that those lips, which I knew all men had touched, touched finally my own, partly in love and partly in articulation of myself and herself, while thus we were the same, though in evil.

On the whole, however, the festival in Venice was dull and unpleasant to the memory, which is certainly our only reality, apart from instant pain or instant pleasure.

The letters of Giacomo Puccini. Farewell to Munich. A single scene from the ballet of the French postcards is hardly enough to establish a tradition of sterility for writers of prose, and certainly not enough to restore Baudelaire to the pavement in Paris. However, the eyes of Maupassant remain to this day the eyes of a Christian saint. The swift gliding of the river Seine is no parallel, but it will do. There is imitation in anything any man may do, and in the matter of escaping loneliness the imitation is pathetically obvious and tawdry.

We have a pretty slick continuity, one man, and

then another, one dead thought emerging from another dead thought; time passing, the Pacific washing away the hours. Days spent with something female of mortal substance, in the sun, by the sea, beneath trees, amid talk.

The tide of heaven, if we were to trouble about it, swells daily to the very door of our lives, yet we walk generally to the seashore to hear the whisper of our monotony; our beloved waves drown the clear fluids of silence and we stand awake and alive.

In 1918 jazz arrived. It existed always, but in 1918 it reached music where it was emphasized. It is wrong to blame the war for this. A school of minnows, darting in a shallow stream, is jazz. A school of tired office girls, darting in a deep tub of New York ooze, is also jazz. The very small difference is not worth noticing: the minnows live in the water naturally, while the girls perish in it naturally, and whatever happens is to be accepted as proper under the circumstances. If prosperity is preferable, this is what to expect.

The fertile soil of the valley was the bed of vine roots, the fountain where they drank. I remembered (in the fiction room) how when, as it sometimes happened, I clipped off a good twig, a twig which would have borne fruit, I would feel guilty of a spiritual misdemeanor, and would therefore ask the vine, as one might ask a mother whose child one has unintentionally hurt, to forgive me. This would happen apart from speech, apart from actual articulation, but it would happen just the same. It would be because I could not bear to destroy a decent thing without experiencing regret, without begging forgiveness.

BIG VALLEY VINEYARD

Again the vines were green with foliage and all the Armenians were going in their automobiles to the vineyards and gathering the tenderest leaves for the spring feasts. The children, born in California, stood among the vines, plucking the young leaves, holding dozens of them in their hands, speaking in Armenian. The leaf of the vine is a food, and the taste is never to be forgotten, even by those who are not Armenians. To Armenians the taste is the very taste of Armenia, and by eating the food each spring all Armenians, wherever they may be, declare to God and Armenia that they have remained loyal. Gathering the leaves of the vine is no small matter, and it is not purely an affair of the table.

For the present, we may presume that the war is beginning to be over, years after the dead have been counted and plans for a new war made, but alas it is not so, and the war is nowhere near beginning to be over. There is no longer any noise (except in the moving pictures of the war, in which the war is being waged all over again; this time on behalf of art), but the unbrave soldiers who have survived are just beginning to cry out because they were forced to be unbrave, because they were unmanned, loosened, driven mad.

All the remaining vices remain unknown, and the dawn, during which man is ill, the dawn of experimentation occurs. There is no sorrow, there is no joy, there is no more than the asking about sorrow and joy. Drama is impossible because everyone is interested in himself, as an experiment, and will not therefore perform any rash act for its own sake, as an inevitability, and the result is that no man can be jealous of any woman, or vice versa. The blurring of specific character among universal precepts is whole, and man, the individualist, is a lie for the next generation. Man is a document, the subject of bad poems. There is no dignity anywhere, not even among peasants, they having been slowly introduced to the vulgarity of modern conveniences, contraceptives, civil rights, etc. They having been taught to read the newspapers. The aspects of experimentation are few. Man is awake, he knows he is awake, he denies destiny, he wishes to observe and he wishes above all things to observe himself. This brings about a state of irresponsibility, Pirandello aiding.

To seek the sane men is to walk alone, sadly.

Working with the peons, though, I kept in touch with the earth. And I picked up a little Mexican.

The most notorious event of history, if one is thoughtful about such occurrences, was not the crucifixion of Christ, but the discovery of America. The crucifixion resulted in Christianity which at its best has been useful and at its worst a form of romanticism for those not writers. On the other hand, the discovery of America (the continent itself) resulted in the moment we now know, in Lincoln, Tom Sawyer, Hollywood, Hearst, and the NRA. Other consequences are innumerable, and if one is to choose between a man and a continent, one must be a materialist not to choose the man; still, it is distressing to try to be a Christian when the name enjoys such capitalistic disgrace, when the greatest Christian church is so fat, so purely ornamental, and so statistical about the soul.

I refer, finally, to the vineyard, from which I have come. I refer, as a last word of these days on earth, to the soil which I have known and which has known me and in which I was nourished.

We had quarrels, of course; the peons and myself and the Greek Stepan, but mostly our conversations were of eternal things, shadows and so on. Stepan, who worked against his better judgment, being by birth a gambler, was nevertheless able to regard his labor in the vineyard as worth the time involved. Twenty years from now, he said, for this work my chin shall be firmer, and my hand, in dealing the cards, shall be swifter, which is important, since I shall have to cheat.

Also Rubio, the tall peon, spoke, but only when silence became too burdensome for him. He was interested mostly in food, fearing, more than death, starvation. One day he asked: What do you eat, you Armenian people? and I told him we ate grape leaves. I myself, I said, eat bread and print. He could not understand how a man could eat print, so I explained to him that food was used by man to nourish the soul, but that in doing so it also stimulated the basest of passions, and that therefore it was advisable to use any substitute that accomplished the end more artfully. And, I said, compared with print no substitute is worth talking about, certainly not love.

Ah, he replied in serious Mexican, you people who read books . . . ah, I cannot be like you. How do you do it?

In the great fiction room of the public library I used to remember the vineyard under the sun, and our talk of eternal things.

Aspirin Is a Member of the N.R.A.

Remember above all things the blood, remember that man is flesh, that flesh suffers pain, and that the mind being caught in flesh suffers with it. Remember that the spirit is a form of the flesh, and the soul its shadow. Above all things humor and intelligence, and truth as the only beginning: not what is said or done, not obviousness: the truth of silences, the intelligence of nothing said, nothing done. The piety. Faces. Memory, our memory of the earth, this one and the other, the one which is now this and the one that was once another, what we saw, and the sun. It is our life and we have no other. Remember God, the multitudinous God.

Remember laughter.

There were nights, in New York, when my hair would freeze on my head, and I would awaken from sleeplessness and remember. I would remember stalking through print, the quiet oratory of some forgotten name, a quiet man who put something down on paper: *yea* and *yea* and *yea*. Something wordless but precise, my hair frozen, and the small attic room in the heart of Manhattan, across the street from the Paramount Building, and myself in the room, in the darkness, alone, waiting for morning. I used to leave my bed sometimes and smoke a cigarette in the darkness. The light I disliked, so I used to sit in the darkness, remembering.

One or two faces I saw coming across the Continent: the boy with a bad dose, riding in the bus, going home to his mother, taking a bad dose with him from a South American resort, talking about the girl, just a young kid and very beautiful, and God, what a pain, every moment and nothing to do about it. He was eighteen or nineteen, and he had gone down to South America to sleep with a girl, and now he had got it, where it hurt most, and he was drinking whisky and swallowing aspirin, to keep him going, to deaden the pain. York, Pennsylvania, a good town, and his people living there. Everything, he said, everything will be all right the minute I get home. And the sick girl, going back to Chicago, talking in her sleep. The language of fear, the articulation of death, no grammar, exclamations, one after another, the midnight grief, children emerging from the grown girl, talking.

OF THE N.R.A.

And the faces of people in the streets, in the large cities and in the small towns, the sameness.

I used to get up in the middle of the night and remember. It was no use trying to sleep, because I was in a place that did not know me, and whenever I tried to sleep the room would declare its strangeness and I would sit up in bed and look into the darkness.

Sometimes the room would hear me laughing softly. I could never cry, because I was doing what I wanted to do, so I couldn't help laughing once in a while, and I would always feel the room listening. Strange fellow, this fellow, I would hear the room say; in this agony, he gets up, with his hair frozen, in the middle of the night, and he laughs.

There was enough pain everywhere, in everyone who lived. If you tried to live a godly life, it didn't make any difference, and in the end you came up with a dull pain in your body and a soul burning with a low fire, eating its substance slowly. I used to think about the pain and in the end all I could do was laugh. If there had been a war, it would have been much easier, more reasonable. The pain would have been explicable. We are fighting for high ideals, we are protecting our homes, we are protecting civilization, and all that. A tangible enemy, a reasonable opposition, and swift pain, so that you couldn't have time enough to think about it much: either it got you all the way, carrying you over into death and calm, or it didn't get you. Also, something tangible to hate, a precise enemy. But without a war it was different. You might try hating God, but in the end you couldn't do it. In the end you laughed softly or you prayed, using pious and blasphemous language.

I used to sit in the dark room, waiting for morning and the fellowship of passengers of the subway. The room had great strength. It belonged. It was part of the place. Fellows like me could come and go, they could die and be born again, but the room was steady and static, always there. I used to feel its indifference toward me, but I could never feel unfriendly toward it. It was part of the scheme, a small attic room in the heart of Manhattan, without an outside window, four dollars a week: me or the next fellow, any of us, it didn't matter. But whenever I laughed, the room would be puzzled, a bit annoyed. It would wonder what there was for me to laugh about, my hair frozen, and my spirit unable to rest.

Sometimes, during the day, shaving, I used to look into the small mirror and see the room in my face, trying to understand me. I would be laughing, looking at the room in the mirror, and it would be annoyed, wondering how I could laugh, what I saw in my life that was amusing.

It was the secrecy that amused me, the fact of my being one of the six million people in the city, living there, waiting to die. I could die in this room, I used to say to myself, and no one would ever understand what had happened, no one would ever say, Do you know that boy from California, the fellow who is studying the subway? Well, he died in a little room on Forty-fourth Street the other night, alone. They found him in the little room, dead. No one would be able to say anything about me if I died, no one knew I was from California and that I was studying the subway, making notes about the people riding in the subway. My presence in Manhattan was not known, so if I came to vanish, my vanishing would not be known. It was a secret, and it amused me. I used to get up in the middle of the night and laugh about it quietly, disturbing the room.

I used to make the room very angry, laughing, and one night it said to me, You are in a hurry but I am not: I shall witness your disintegration, but when you are destroyed I shall be standing here quietly. You will see.

It made me laugh. I knew it was the truth, but it was amusing to me. I couldn't help laughing at the room wanting to see me go down.

But there was an armistice: what happened was this: I moved away. I rented another room. It was a war without a victor. I packed my things and moved to the Mills Hotel.

But it isn't so easy to escape a war. A war has a way of following a man around, and my room in the Mills Hotel was even more malicious than the other. It was smaller and therefore its eloquence was considerably louder. Its walls used to fall in upon me, with the whiteness of madness, but I went on laughing. In the middle of the night I used to hear my neighbors, old and young men. I used to hear them speaking out against life from their sleep. I used to hear much weeping. That year many men were weeping from their sleep. I used to laugh about this. It was such a startling thing that I used to laugh. The worst that can happen to any of us, I used to laugh, is death. It is a small thing. Why are you men weeping?

It was because of remembrance, I suppose. Death is always in a man, but sometimes life is in him so strongly that it makes a sad remembrance and comes out in the form of weeping through sleep.

And it was because of the pain. Everybody was in pain. I was studying the subway and I could see the pain in the faces of everybody. I looked everywhere for one face that was not the mask of a pained life, but I did not find such a face. It was this that made my study of the subway so fascinating. After months of study I reached a decision about all of us in Manhattan. It was this: the subway is death, all of us are riding to death. No catastrophe, no horrible accident: only slow death, emerging from life. It was such a terrific fact that I had to laugh about it.

I lived in many rooms, in many sections of the city, East Side, West Side, downtown, uptown, Harlem, the Bronx, Brooklyn, all over the place. It was the same everywhere, my hair frozen at night, alien walls around me, and the smile of death in my eyes.

But I didn't mind. It was what I had wanted to do. I was a clerk in one of thousands of offices of a great national enterprise, doing my part to make America the most prosperous nation on earth, more millionaires per square inch than all the other nations put together, etc. I was paying cash for my sleeplessness, for the privilege of riding in the subway. I was eating in the Automats, renting vacant rooms all over the place, buying clothes, newspapers, aspirin.

I do not intend to leave aspirin out of this document. It is too important to leave out. It is the hero of this story, all of us six million people in New York, swallowing it, day after day. All of us in pain, needing it. Aspirin is an evasion. But so is life. The way we live it. You take aspirin in order to keep going. It deadens pain. It helps you to sleep. It keeps you aboard the subway. It is a substitute for the sun, for strong blood. It stifles remembrance, silences weeping.

It does not harm the heart. That is what the manufacturers say. They say it is absolutely harmless. Maybe it is. Death does not harm the heart either. Death is just as harmless as aspirin. I expect casket manufacturers to make this announcement in the near future. I expect to see a full page advertisement in the *Saturday Evening Post,* making a slogan on behalf of death. *Do not be deceived . . . die and see your dreams come true . . . death does not harm the heart . . . it is absolutely harmless . . . doctors everywhere recommend it . . .* and so on.

You hear a lot of sad talk about all the young men who died in the Great War. Well, what about this war? Is it less real because it destroys with less violence, with a ghastlier shock, with a more sustained pain?

The coming of snow in Manhattan is lovely. All the ugliness is softened by the pious whiteness. But with the snow comes the deadly cold. With the snow death comes a little closer to everyone. If you are pretty rich, it doesn't bother you much: you don't have to get up in the morning in a cold room and rush out to an Automat for a cup of coffee and then dive into the subway. If you are rich, the snow is only beautiful to you. You get up when you please, and there is nothing to do but sit in warm rooms and talk with other rich people. But if you aren't rich, if you are working to make America a nation of prosperous millionaires, then the snow is both beautiful and ghastly. And when the cold of the snow gets into your bones you are apt to forget that it is beautiful; you are apt to notice only that it is ghastly.

A few evenings ago I was listening to the radio, out here in San Francisco. Aspirin days are over for me. I depend on the sun these days. I was listening to a very good program, sponsored by one of America's most prosperous manufacturers of aspirin. You know the name. I do not intend to advertise the company. It does enough advertising of its own. The radio announcer said the cold and sore throat season had come, and of course it had. I could see snow falling over Manhattan, increasing the sales of aspirin all over the city. Then the announcer said, Aspirin is a member of the N.R.A.

It made me laugh to hear that. But it is the truth. Aspirin *is* a member of the N.R.A. It *is* helping everyone to evade fundamentals, it *is* helping to keep people going to work. Aspirin *is* helping to bring back prosperity. It *is* doing its part. It *is* sending millions of half-dead people to their jobs. It *is* doing a great deal to keep the spirit of this nation from disintegrating. It *is* deadening pain everywhere. It *isn't* preventing anything, but it is deadening pain.

What about the N.R.A.? Well, I leave that to you.

OF THE N.R.A.

Maybe the N.R.A. is a member of aspirin. Anyhow, together they make a pretty slick team. They are deadening a lot of pain, but they aren't preventing any pain. Everything is the same everywhere.

All I know is this: that if you keep on taking aspirin long enough it will cease to deaden pain.

And that is when the fun begins. That is when you begin to notice that snow isn't beautiful at all. That is when your hair begins to freeze and you begin to get up in the middle of the night, laughing quietly, waiting for the worst, remembering all the pain and not wanting to evade it any longer, not wanting any longer to be half-dead, wanting full death or full life. That is when you begin to be mad about the way things are going in this country, the way things are with life, with man. That is when, weak as you are, something old and savage and defiant in you comes up bitterly out of your illness and starts to smash things, making a path for you to the sun, destroying cities, wrecking subways, pushing you into the sun, getting you away from evasions, dragging you by your neck to life.

It made me laugh, the way I used to laugh in New York, when I heard that radio announcer say that aspirin was a member of the N.R.A., and it made me remember. It made me want to say what I knew about aspirin.

Seventeen

Sam Wolinsky was seventeen, and a month had passed since he had begun to shave; now he was in love. And he wanted to do something. A feeling of violence was in him, and he was thinking of himself as something enormous in the world. He felt drunk with strength that had accumulated from the first moment of his life to the moment he was now living, and he felt almost insane because of the strength. Death was nothing. It could not matter if he died; feeling as he did, it could not matter. All that mattered was this moment, Wolinsky in love, alive, walking down Ventura Avenue, in America, Wolinsky of the universe, the crazy Polak with the broken nose.

Everything was small, beneath his enormity, and he was seeking something to do, some cruelty; it was godly to be cruel, to hurt, even to destroy. It was proper to mock soft feelings in man, to stand by, laughing at the pettiness of man. There was no sacred thing in the world. He knew; he was certain; everything was made in a profane way, and there was no sense in trying to change ugly things into lovely things, no use being dishonest.

He was in love and there was no girl. He was in love with female whiteness, the swelling of female parts, the curve of back, the soft cohesion of limbs uniting in wholeness, hair, smile or strong frown as of passion, female motion, woman, but mostly the idea of woman. He felt no tenderness, and he had no wish to imitate the moving-picture males, touching the females. That was fake. It was fraudulence. They were trying to keep people unaware of the truth, making it a soft event, a thing of no strength. They were trying to hide the animal drive in man, the lust to function violently, but they couldn't fool him, Wolinsky. And the love songs: all rot. And the male weeping: disgusting. A man had to be alone, something by himself. Always a man had to be above occurrences; he had to stand up and laugh at the way things happened, the inevitable way.

He was a slight boy with sad Polish eyes, small for his age, fidgety, a lover of books, loud in conversation. At thirteen he began to read books that were said to be evil, books with thoughts in them that were said to be vile, about women, Schopenhauer, and reading these books he began to expand, growing large inwardly. He became disdainful, aloof, mocking, and he made impolite remarks to his school teachers, shocking them, seeking trouble everywhere, a chance to quarrel, to be angry, a chance not to be passive and indifferent and half-asleep about life. It was all excessive nervousness, and it came partly from the books he read and partly from himself, the way he was, inevitably, insane with life.

Nevertheless, there was a strange tenderness in him that he could never efface, and every now and then he would stare at himself in a mirror and see the tenderness in his eyes. It would make him frantic. He didn't want to be that way. He didn't want to be weak like other people. He was proud because he hadn't once cried in ten years. And he knew there had been many occasions for him to cry. The time he struck his father and felt inwardly unclean. It was never for himself that he had wanted to cry; for others, for hurting something in them, but he had always made himself laugh.

All his life he had wanted to be fully alive, physically, violently, and now he was beginning to feel what it was like. The feeling of vastness in him, the sense of unlimited strength, the mockery in his heart for sacred things, the ribaldry that he felt in regard to love. Love? He knew all about that nonsense. He had read an article in *The Haldeman-Julius Monthly* about love, and he knew. Love was purely physical; all the rest was imaginary, stupid, fake. Strength accumulated in man and had to be released. It was not personal; it was abstract, universal. One woman was the same as another; it was the function, the act that was inevitable.

Any man who got soft inside about the lust that was in him was a fool. Any man who felt shame was a fool. Man was thus, the chemical situation was thus, there was nothing else to it. And the married women in church, singing, it was laughable: Freud said they were merely doing in a very subtle way what they dared not even think of doing: fornicating. Pathetic and amusing, pious ladies committing spiritual adultery in church, on Sunday. It was a fine thing to know, to laugh about. There was at least some godliness in being truthful, even if a man had to be a little vulgar.

There was no girl. All his life something had kept him apart. He had felt love for certain girls in school, but something had kept him apart from them. First it was a feeling that he was unworthy. This feeling was mingled with a consciousness of prejudice against his race. To the others he was a Polak, nothing, nobody. Then it was timidity, then pride, and ever since it had remained pride. He could walk alone. He did not need to humiliate himself by asking a girl to be interested in him, wanting her body and all the rest of it. The soul. The part that really didn't exist, according to science and *The Haldeman-Julius Monthly,* but somehow seemed always to be there in girls. The way they looked at things, the way they came out of their eyes, dancing or being naked or running violently, or weeping. He had seen the girls emerging from their eyes, and it had been very subtle, but he had understood the innate structure of each girl, the specific manner of motion. And always he had preferred the ones who had left themselves violently.

He was a bit mad; he was certain of it, but it never worried him and he was never ashamed. It was out of the accumulated strength in him that his madness emerged in his conduct. One day, walking, he struck a telephone post with his fist, and the knuckles bled and his fist became swollen with pain, but he was not ashamed. He had been walking along, feeling expansive and large, and suddenly he had done it, not thinking about it one way or another. That was all: something to do, some cruelty. The post might have been a man, or life, or God, the idea of these things. It might have been all men, man. He had simply struck. A hurt fist was nothing. Inside he had felt exhilarated. He had laughed, shaking his hand with the pain, laughing about it.

And his fights with other boys; they had always refreshed him. The least little thing would make him fight, and he didn't care how large a boy might be. All he wanted was to function with strength, violently, to let himself out. They had broken his nose twice, but he hadn't felt sorry. He was only a Polak. Physically, he was small. His features were hardly masculine. He knew all about these things. But inside; nobody could say that he wasn't a man. He had taken pains to prove it. All his life he had taken pains to be stronger, braver than his fellows. He had been one of the first boys to begin smoking cigarettes at Longfellow School. He had been thirteen at the time. All the same, there was this old tenderness in him, and it was inexplicable.

SEVENTEEN

It was Sunday afternoon, September, and he was walking down Ventura Avenue, on his way to town. It was thick in him, the old lust, only in a new way: something besides fighting, striking things, a maddening sexual feeling, a desire for the universe, a desire to attack and violate it, to make his reality specific, to establish his presence on earth. He felt no need to apologize for the bawdy feeling that was in him. It was not his fault. He hadn't established the basis of the universe, the manner of life, the method of remaining sane.

He met many friends in Court House Park where the afternoon band concert was being held, boys who feared and respected him, but secretly disliked him. He knew they did not like him. He had no friends. He was alone. He disliked the town; it was small and petty, full of the weaknesses of man. He felt himself to be a stranger in the place. And these boys who greeted him were merely the boys with whom he had grown up. They were in the park because of the girls, the girls with whom they had grown up. What they were doing was pathetic. Woman to him was more than the girls of his time. She was something primarily evil, something vast, eternal and ungiggling. All these girls were full of giggles. They giggled every time a boy looked at them. He walked about in the park, listening to the music in the summer air, watching the boys trying to make the girls, feeling the lust growing in him; then he left the park and began to walk toward Chinatown.

There were some whores over there; he heard the music fading away, the town dwindling away from his mind with the music. He crossed the Southern Pacific tracks on Tulare Street, and began to walk among the Mexicans and Hindus and Chinese of Chinatown. The place was filthy with a filth that was man's, but he had never been squeamish. The player-piano of the Lyceum Theatre was making a nervous racket, and a crowd of Mexicans and Negroes was standing in front of the theatre, eating peanuts and sunflower seeds, talking loudly. He saw one Mexican face that somehow angered him, the face itself, and for a moment he wanted to start a fight. It was strange: something unclean in man that had found expression in the face, and he wanted to object to the face physically. And the musical, sing-song Mexican talk; it annoyed him. It was too soft and effortless, not hard and solid like English, not precise. He wondered where the women could be, and he walked up a block to F Street. On the corner, a poolroom full of Chinese and Mexicans, much smoke, and no sight of female face or figure.

He began to look up second-story windows, seeking some sign of professional evil. He saw red flower pots on window sills with sickly geranium plants growing out of them, and suddenly he began to feel that he was going around like a dog in heat. It made him sick to have such a feeling about himself, and yet he did not want to evade the truth. It was something like that, what he was doing. There was something of the low animal in it, and he hadn't had such a feeling before.

He wanted to be honest. He had come over to Chinatown to have a woman. He hadn't had the thought in his mind in a secretive way; it hadn't been in the background of his mind in the form of a vague possibility. It had been specific, outright. He would never be able to maintain his belief in himself if he did not go through with it. He began to look around for certain doorways, passageways leading to such places, small hotels. Nothing looked evil. Nothing seemed vast and universal and strong. The doorways of small hotels were exactly like other doorways. It was incredible. He wasn't seeking something pathetic. He wanted genuine evil, clean and large and bawdy. And all that he saw was narrowness and uncleanliness, and it all reflected the dirt and weakness of man, his essential cheapness. He wanted to fight somebody, but recognized the wish as a subtle evasion and refused to entertain the thought.

It was not a question of doing something with his fists; it was a question of finding out definitely about evil, whether or not it was in man to be really strong, or if it was essential for him to be something eternally small and maudlin. He felt this truth cleanly, accurately.

Scrambling up the stairs of a small hotel, he remembered himself suddenly scrambling up the stairs of a small hotel in Chinatown and he remembered how suddenly, how secretively, he had turned into the passageway.

He stood in the hallway of the hotel, looking about, absorbing the filthiness of the place, not the mere physical filthiness, the rotten odor, the ugliness of the walls, the low ceiling, but the symbolic filthiness of the hotel, the whole idea of it. There was a table in a corner with a small hand-bell on it, and a sign on the wall, *please ring bell.* He touched the bell and heard it ring, losing his breath. Waiting impatiently, dismissing a wish to run down the stairs and escape, he began to notice that there was no laughter, nothing of the universal about what was going on.

He heard walking in the hall, soft slippers shuffling over soft carpet, and the sound was pathetic to him. Some common human being was moving toward him; that was all. He heard no sound of strong, godly evil, no laughter. And suddenly he was facing a small woman of fifty with hair on her upper lip, a white hag, and he was looking into her unclean eyes; no evil—filthiness.

He wanted to speak but could not. "I want," he began to say, then gulped and felt ashamed of himself. Then he wished to efface this woman from the earth, to have her politely out of his way, out of all life: her dirt, the rot of her age. Then he did what he believed to be a cowardly thing, the most cowardly thing he had ever done. He smiled. He permitted himself to smile, when as a matter of fact he did not wish to smile at all, when as a matter of fact he wished even to destroy the very idea of this person standing before him, and he knew that his smile must be weak and fake and pathetic.

The smile told what he wanted. "Follow me, honey," said the woman, leading him down the hall. Honey? he thought. From this hag? This sort of weakness and fraudulence, and from this sort of person?

The old woman opened the door of a room, and he

went in and sat down. "I'll send a girl right over," said the old woman, going away.

Then he saw himself from away up in the firmament sitting pathetically in a small room, smoking a cigarette, feeling unclean, dirty in every moment of his life, from the first moment to this moment, but refusing to get up and go away, wanting to know, one way or another, strength or weakness, laughter or no laughter.

A half hour later, a mere half hour, he was going down the stairs, remembering all the rotten details, the face, the hands, the body, the way it happened. And the ghastly silence as of death, the absence of strength, the impossibility of laughter, the true ugliness of it.

He fled from Chinatown, delirious with anger and shock and horror. He saw the earth flat and drab, cheap and pointless, and what was worse he saw himself as he was, small, the size of a small man, and cheap and pointless and drab and ungodly, and everything despicable. He wanted to laugh at himself but could not. He wanted to laugh at the whole world, the fraudulence of all things that had life and motion, but could not. He began to walk in the city, not knowing which way to go, not understanding why he was there at all, walking, dreading the thought of ever again going home, and all that he could think of was the ghastly filthiness of truth even, the everlasting pettiness of man, the whole falsity of humanity.

He walked a long while, and at last he went home, entering his father's house. And when he was asked to eat, he said that he was not hungry, and he went to his room and took a book and tried to read. The words were on the pages as evasions, like everything else. He closed the book and tried just sitting and not thinking, but it was impossible.

He could not get over the feeling of the cheapness of the whole thing, the absence of strength, the absence of dignity, the impossibility of laughter.

His mother, worrying, standing at the door of his room, heard him crying. At first she could not believe it, but afterwards she knew that it was real crying, like her own crying sometimes, and she went to the boy's father. "He is in there alone, crying," she said to her husband. "Sammy, our boy, is crying, papa. Sammy. Please go to him, papa. I am afraid. Please see why he is crying." And the poor woman began herself to cry. It made her very happy to cry over her son crying. It made her feel that at last he was like all of them, small and pathetic, a real baby, her boy, and she kept on repeating, "Papa, Sammy is crying; he is crying, papa."

A Cold Day

Dear M—,
I want you to know that it is very cold in San Francisco today, and that I am freezing. It is so cold in my room that every time I start to write a short story the cold stops me and I have to get up and do bending exercises. It means, I think, that something's got to be done about keeping short story writers warm. Sometimes when it is very cold I am able to do very good writing, but at other times I am not. It is the same when the weather is excessively pleasant. I very much dislike letting a day go by without writing a short story and that is why I am writing this letter: to let you know that I am very angry about the weather. Do not think that I am sitting in a nice warm room

in sunny California, as they call it, and making up all this stuff about the cold. I am sitting in a very cold room and there is no sun anywhere, and the only thing I can talk about is the cold because it is the only thing going on today. I am freezing and my teeth are chattering. I would like to know what the Democratic party ever did for freezing short story writers. Everybody else gets heat. We've got to depend on the sun and in the winter the sun is undependable. That's the fix I am in: wanting to write and not being able to, because of the cold.

One winter day last year the sun came out and its light came into my room and fell across my table, warming my table and my room and warming me. So I did some brisk bending exercises and then sat down and began to write a short story. But it was a winter day and before I had written the first paragraph of the story the sun had fallen back behind clouds and there I was in my room, sitting in the cold, writing a story. It was such a good story that even though I knew it would never be printed I had to go on writing it, and as a result I was frozen stiff by the time I finished writing it. My face was blue and I could barely move my limbs, they were so cold and stiff. And my room was full of the smoke of a package of Chesterfield cigarettes, but even the smoke was frozen. There were clouds of it in my room, but my room was very cold just the same. Once, while I was writing, I thought of getting a tub and making a fire in it. What I intended to do was to burn a half dozen of my books and keep warm, so that I could write my story. I found an old tub and I brought it to my room, but when I looked around for books to burn I couldn't find any. All of my books are old and cheap. I have about five hundred of them and I paid a nickel each for most of them, but when I looked around for titles to burn, I couldn't find any. There was a large heavy book in German on anatomy that would have made a swell fire, but when I opened it and read a line of that beautiful language, *sie bestehen aus zwei Hüftgelenkbeugemuskeln des Oberschenkels, von denen der eine breitere,* and so on, I couldn't do it. It was asking too much. I couldn't understand the language, I couldn't understand a word in the whole book, but it was somehow too eloquent to use for a fire. The book had cost me five cents two or three years ago, and it weighed about six pounds, so you see that even as fire wood it had been a bargain and I should have been able to tear out its pages and make a fire.

But I couldn't do it. There were over a thousand pages in the book and I planned to burn one page at a time and see the fire of each page, but when I thought of all that print being effaced by fire and all that accurate language being removed from my library, I couldn't do it, and I still have the book. When I get tired of reading great writers, I go to this book and read language that I cannot understand, *während der Kindheit ist sie von birnförmiger Gestalt und liegt vorzugsweise in der Bauchhöhle.* It is simply blasphemous to think of burning a thousand pages of such language. And of course I haven't so much as mentioned the marvelous illustrations.

Then I began to look around for cheap fiction.

And you know the world is chock full of such stuff.

Nine books out of ten are cheap worthless fiction, inorganic stuff. I thought, well, there are at least a half dozen of those books in my library and I can burn them and be warm and write my story. So I picked out six books and together they weighed about as much as the German anatomy book. The first was *Tom Brown At Oxford: A Sequel to School Days At Rugby,* Two Volumes in One. The first book had 378 pages, and the second 430, and all these pages would have made a small fire that would have lasted a pretty long time, but I had never read the book and it seemed to me that I had no right to burn a book I hadn't even read. It looked as if it ought to be a book of cheap prose, one worthy of being burned, but I couldn't do it. I read, *The belfry-tower rocked and reeled, as that peal rang out, now merry, now scornful, now plaintive, from those narrow belfry windows, into the bosom of the soft southwest wind, which was playing round the old gray tower of Englebourn church.* Now that isn't exactly tremendous prose, but it isn't such very bad prose either. So I put the book back on the shelf.

The next book was *Inez: A Tale of the Alamo,* and it was dedicated to The Texan Patriots. It was by the author of another book called *Beulah,* and yet another called *St. Elmo.* The only thing I knew about this writer or her books was that one day a girl at school had been severely reprimanded for bringing to class a book called *St. Elmo.* It was said to be the sort of book that would corrupt the morals of a young girl. Well, I opened the book and read, *I am dying; and, feeling as I do, that few hours are allotted me, I shall not hesitate to speak freely and candidly. Some might think me deviating from the delicacy of my sex; but, under the circumstances, I feel that I am not. I have loved you long, and to know that my love is returned, is a source of deep and unutterable joy to me.* And so on.

This was such bad writing that it was good, and I decided to read the whole book at my first opportunity. There is much for a young writer to learn from our poorest writers. It is very destructive to burn bad books, almost more destructive than to burn good ones.

The next book was *Ten Nights In A Bar Room, and What I Saw There* by T. S. Arthur. Well, even this book was too good to burn. The other three books were by Hall Caine, Brander Matthews, and Upton Sinclair. I had read only Mr. Sinclair's book, and while I didn't like it a lot as a piece of writing, I couldn't burn it because the print was so fine and the binding so good. Typographically it was one of my best books.

Anyway, I didn't burn a single page of a single book, and I went on freezing and writing. Every now and then I burned a match just to remind myself what a flame looked like, just to keep in touch with the idea of heat and warmth. It would be when I wanted to light another cigarette and instead of blowing out the flame I would let it burn all the way down to my fingers.

It is simply this: that if you have any respect for the mere idea of books, what they stand for in life, if you believe in paper and print, you cannot burn any page of any book. Even if you are freezing. Even if you are trying to do a bit of writing yourself. You can't do it. It is asking too much.

Today it is as cold in my room as the day I wanted to make a fire of books. I am sitting in the cold, smoking cigarettes, and trying to get this coldness onto paper so that when it becomes warm again in San Francisco I won't forget how it was on the cold days.

I have a small phonograph in my room and I play it when I want to exercise in order to keep warm. Well, when it gets to be very cold in my room this phonograph won't work. Something goes wrong inside, the grease freezes and the wheels won't turn, and I can't have music while I am bending and swinging my arms. I've got to do it without music. It is much more pleasant to exercise with jazz, but when it is very cold the phonograph won't work and I am in a hell of a fix. I have been in here since eight o'clock this morning and it is now a quarter to five, and I am in a hell of a mess. I hate to let a day go by without doing something about it, without saying something, and all day I have been in here with my books that I never read, trying to get started and I haven't gotten anywhere. Most of the time I have been walking up and down the room (two steps in any direction brings you to a wall) and bending and kicking and swinging my arms. That's practically all I have been doing. I tried the phonograph a half dozen times to see if the temperature hadn't gone up a little, but it hadn't, and the phonograph wouldn't play music.

I thought I ought to tell you about this. It's nothing important. It's sort of silly, making so much of a little cold weather, but at the same time the cold is a fact today and it is the big thing right now and I am speaking of it. The thing that amazes and pleases me is that my typewriter hasn't once clogged today. Around Christmas when we had a very cold spell out here it was always clogging, and the more I oiled it the more it clogged. I couldn't do a thing with it. The reason was that I had been using the wrong kind of oil. But all this time that I have been writing about the cold my typewriter has been doing its work excellently, and this amazes and pleases me. To think that in spite of the cold this machine can go right on making the language I use is very fine. It encourages me to stick with it, whatever happens. If the machine will work, I tell myself, then you've got to work with it. That's what it amounts to. If you can't write a decent short story because of the cold, write something else. Write anything. Write a long letter to somebody. Tell them how cold you are. By the time the letter is received the sun will be out again and you will be warm again, but the letter will be there mentioning the cold. If it is so cold that you can't make up a little ordinary Tuesday prose, why, what the hell, say anything that comes along, just so it's the truth. Talk about your toes freezing, about the time you actually wanted to burn books to keep warm but couldn't do it, about the phonograph. Speak of the little unimportant things on a cold day, when your mind is numb and your feet and hands frozen. Mention the things you wanted to write but couldn't. This is what I have been telling myself.

After coffee this morning, I came here to write an

important story. I was warm with the coffee and I didn't realize how really cold it was. I brought out paper and started to line up what I was going to say in this important story that will never be written because once I lose a thing I lose it forever, this story that is forever lost because of the cold that got into me and silenced me and made me jump up from my chair and do bending exercises. Well, I can tell you about it. I can give you an idea what it was to have been like. I remember that much about it, but I didn't write it and it is lost. It will give you something of an idea as to how I write.

I will tell you the things I was telling myself this morning while I was getting this story lined up in my mind:

Think of America, I told myself this morning. The whole thing. The cities, all the houses, all the people, the coming and going, the coming of children, the going of them, the coming and going of men and death, and life, the movement, the talk, the sound of machinery, the oratory, think of the pain in America and the fear and the deep inward longing of all things alive in America. Remember the great machines, wheels turning, smoke and fire, the mines and the men working them, the noise, the confusion. Remember the newspapers and the moving picture theatres and everything that is a part of this life. Let this be your purpose: to suggest this great country.

Then turn to the specific. Go out to some single person and dwell with him, within him, lovingly, seeking to understand the miracle of his being, and utter the truth of his existence and reveal the splendor of the mere fact of his being alive, and say it in great prose, simply, show that he is of the time, of the machines and the fire and smoke, the newspapers and the noise. Go with him to his secret and speak of it gently, showing that it is the secret of man. Do not deceive. Do not make up lies for the sake of pleasing anyone. No one need be killed in your story. Simply relate what is the great event of all history, of all time, the humble, artless truth of mere being. There is no greater theme: no one need be violent to help you with your art. There *is* violence. Mention it of course when it is time to mention it. Mention the war. Mention all ugliness, all waste. Do even this lovingly. But emphasize the glorious truth of mere being. It is the major theme. You do not have to create a triumphant climax. The man you write of need not perform some heroic or monstrous deed in order to make your prose great. Let him do what he has always done, day in and day out, continuing to live. Let him walk and talk and think and sleep and dream and awaken and walk again and talk again and move and be alive. It is enough. There is nothing else to write about. You have never seen a short story in life. The events of life have never fallen into the form of the short story or the form of the poem, or into any other form. Your own consciousness is the only form you need. Your own awareness is the only action you need. Speak of this man, recognize his existence. Speak of man.

Well, this is a poor idea of what the story was to have been like. I was warm with coffee when I was telling myself what and how to write, but now I am freezing, and this is the closest I can come to what I had in mind. It was to have been something fine, but now all that I have is this vague remembrance of the story. The least I can do is put into words this remembrance. Tomorrow I will write another story, a different story. I will look at the picture from a different viewpoint. I don't know for sure, but I may feel cocky and I may mock this country and the life that is lived here. It is possible. I can do it. I have done it before, and sometimes when I get mad about political parties and political graft I sit down and mock this great country of ours. I get mean and I make man out to be a rotten, worthless, unclean thing. It isn't man, but I make out as if it is. It's something else, something less tangible, but for mockery it is more convenient to make out that it is man. It's my business to get at the truth, but when you start to mock, you say to hell with the truth. Nobody's telling the truth, why should I? Everybody's telling nice lies, writing nice stories and novels, why should I worry about the truth. There is no truth. Only grammar, punctuation, and all that rot. But I know better. I can get mad at things and start to mock, but I know better. At its best, the whole business is pretty sad, pretty pathetic.

All day I have been in this room freezing, wanting to say something solid and clean about all of us who are alive. But it was so cold I couldn't do it. All I could do was swing my arms and smoke cigarettes and feel rotten.

Early this morning when I was warm with coffee

A COLD DAY

I had this great story in my mind, ready to get into print, but it got away from me.

The most I can say now is that it is very cold in San Francisco today, and I am freezing.

The Earth, Day, Night, Self

Sitting across the table from him, he listened to the girl talking, telling him something that involved each of them, something that had begun in him years ago and would never end, something in man . . . about the earth, being alive on it, going through days and nights, being something with substance and motion, oneself.

From the second-story window he saw a man riding a bicycle in the street . . . two wheels rolling on the levelness of the city and a man on it . . . the girl talking . . .

That must have been the year he had gone with his mother and father to the photographer's, the year he was nearly three. He didn't remember actually going, but he had the photograph, and in it he saw the tall man holding him in his arms, and his mother sitting beside the tall man, all of them smiling. It was the year his father was alive, smiling in the photograph.

The next thing he knew he was holding his mother's hand, walking in the night through the dark city, in the silence. Where are we going? he asked.

He did not remember an answer, and he continued to walk beside his mother, maybe four years old.

Night came and he sent his sadness into his sleep, weeping softly there without shedding tears.

Once he laughed, but it was not like laughing when you were awake. It was much bigger, it meant all sorts of things; it had to do with everything, and in his sleep he was afraid someone might hear him and ask why he was laughing . . . his mother might want to know, and he knew he wouldn't be able to tell her . . . but in his sleep he knew why he was laughing, where the laughter came from, what it meant, but it wasn't in language and it couldn't be said in words. It was there, though, the whole meaning for himself, the whole picture of the earth and man. To make him laugh.

One morning he found himself in a school building, staring at the horror. To teach you to read, he heard. I don't want to read, he wanted to tell them, but he couldn't explain. He knew he didn't need to read; it was all there already, before him, both at night and during the day, and seeing everything he felt no need for the words. The *things* were the words themselves and he had eyes, he was seeing how it was, but they led him to a room full of desks and small boys and girls and they said, What is your name?

Oh, he said. You mean me? That lady, he wanted to say, she, the one that was here and went away, she is my mother. The tall man in the picture, who isn't living any more, he is my father. They call me John. John, he told them. My name is John. The other name is Melovich.

He sat down and forgot what happened for a month.

But the worry got into his sleep. About the other boys in the room, and something they meant to do about him. It was that they were thinking of him, in their own minds, seeing him with their eyes, destroying the secret. They were talking of him, and he didn't want anyone to do that. He wanted wholeness, to be alone solidly, not talked of, not seen, not recognized; but the boys had him in their minds. John, they said, how far is it to China? Of course he didn't know. Then one of the boys got on his hands and knees behind him, and another boy pushed him over, and the whole world went up-side down, and all the boys laughed at him and said: China is all the way around the world, ha ha ha.

Oh, I see, he thought. Games, they mean. I thought they meant China, but they mean to play. If you believe what they ask, if you notice the words, then they push you over, laughing at you. The words are not to be listened to. They are for the game, China, and over you go. I see, he thought. That is it.

Also, the teacher. She was angry about him. She said that he was stupid. It was because he wanted to know, because of the questions he was asking, and she made him stand in the corner. She said, c-a-t is cat, and he said: No, the cat is black hair and whiskers and tail and eyes. That's all he knew, but it made her very angry and she shook him, and all the little boys and girls laughed at him. C-a-t cat, that wasn't so. The four legs walking quietly, that was the cat. Why were they making things up?

The worry got into his sleep, and he brought out the cat in his dream and had it walk before the teacher. There, he said, there is the cat, not what you said. You see? The fur walking, and the eyes.

Then it was night and he was awake, standing in the street, looking up at the dark window of the place where he lived. The front door was locked and no one was in the house. He was in the street, crying. My mother, he said to the people who questioned him, she is not in there. He thought everything was going to fall to pieces, and he felt the bigness of the world, other people alive who were not related to him.

He didn't remember what finally happened. All he remembered was being in the dark street, crying to himself, feeling the whole thing breaking to pieces.

They taught him to read. It was silly, about a dog called Fido. That's all he remembered, a picture of a dog called Fido, and some print spelling words about the things Fido could do. Bark, bow wow, run and play, and so on. It was all pretty stupid, but it was what they were teaching in the school, so he tried to pretend that it made sense, and he tried hard not to ask too many questions.

THE EARTH, DAY, NIGHT, SELF

He was sitting in a dark theatre beside his mother, looking at pictures of people moving quietly at the front of the theatre, touching one another, even with their lips, making faces, running, doing swift things, making a story. Then he saw the sea, and the sea did nothing. It was splendid, big and simple, so easy for him to believe, all that water, standing quietly, no words and no people making faces and running, all the water quietly. And the sea went into him, appearing again in his sleep, vast and lovely and wordless.

It was not easy to talk, even with his mother: it seemed so much more natural to say nothing, even when he was ill or bewildered, and sometimes she would call him to her.

John, are you all right? Why don't you say something? Let me see your tongue. John, is anything the matter?

But all he could do was look into her eyes. Sometimes he would be sick, but it was himself and anything that was himself couldn't be talked about and he would show his mother his tongue and let her hold his hand to see if he had a fever, and when she would say, John, John, you are sick, my poor boy; when she would say this, he would be amazed. That was in her mind, he would feel. She made that up. I'm just standing here. It meant, then, that he was outside, too, everywhere, outside of himself too, in other people's minds. They could see him and being larger they could see him differently from what he knew, and they could come to conclusions that were impossible for him. They could fix him in their minds as so much height and weight, so much face and mind, and a condition; but he couldn't do it. He was merely there, trying to figure it out, waiting.

It was the church then, God in Slavonian, and Jesus. He remembered the people singing, his mother sitting beside him, singing and looking strangely beautiful, something new in her, and a new odor, sweeter now. He wanted to sing with them. It was really beautiful, the Sunday morning light in the church, and everyone singing, but he didn't know the words. The earth was so lovely, it was so splendid to be alive, sitting in the church. Suddenly he began to pour himself out among the people, into the earth, singing with his mother, making up words, unable to remain silent any longer. That was a lovely time, that time in the church, singing because he was alive.

The locomotive came out of nowhere, big and black and the ringing of bells, the turning of steel wheels, making him afraid. John, his mother said, we are going away. They got aboard the train and sat down. He heard the locomotive begin to puff, and very slowly the train began to move, carrying him with it. He was amazed, sitting in the train. He saw the buildings coming to and going away from him, at first slowly, then swifter, and swifter, and swifter, and pretty soon it was like music, one two three, one two three, solid things hurrying by, flash, a tree, a house, flash, and the music, one two three, one and one and two and two, the wheels grinding, a road, a river, flash, flash, and the scream of the locomotive. It was very sad to see so many things for such a little time, before he had even been able to look at them solidly, and the bigness of the place, one thing at a time, stretching out endlessly in all directions, the whole earth, nearly broke his heart. He wanted to touch everything. He wanted to have something to do with all of it. He wanted to be aware of, and to mean something to, everything he saw, every tree, every house, every face, all the earth, all the hills covered with grass and flowers, all the streams. And the house where he had lived with his father and his mother . . . where was that now? And where was he that had lived in that house? That little boy who couldn't learn to read . . .

It was a new place now, no hills, a smaller place, new faces, new streets, and he was still the same, though he was wearing a bigger pair of trousers and a new jacket.

Then it was a dream, carrying him to something new, a newer loveliness, a little girl named Maxine, in the third grade. In the dream he went to her and she saw his love and she loved him. What happened was this: they walked together, holding hands. In the morning, after the dream, he was ill with love for the girl. He could not eat breakfast, and he walked to school in a daze, wishing never to emerge from the dream. When he saw the girl in the classroom he became so ill with love he could barely stand on his legs. She sat two seats in front of him, across the aisle, and all day he sat staring at her soft brown hair, still living in the dream. He forgot that he was at school, and each time he was called on to recite, he could think of nothing to say, there was absolutely nothing to say: all he knew was that he loved the girl, loved her, loved her, nothing else. He wanted nothing other than to know that the girl loved him. He wondered what it could mean. A whole month he loved her secretly. Then she dwindled away, still coming to class but no longer meaning what she had once meant to him.

It was evening, and he was walking across the school grounds on his way home, singing *It's a long long way to Tipperary, it's a long way to go.* He was singing with all his might, and he hadn't seen Miss Fargo coming down the school steps. He had felt that he was alone and that he could shout it out the way he liked, but suddenly he saw her, stopping at the foot of the stairs, looking amazed.

Come here, John, he heard her say, and he went to her, feeling ashamed of the noise he had made. He hadn't known anyone was around. He hadn't meant to let anyone hear him. He stood before her, holding his cap, feeling embarrassed.

Where is Tipperary, John? she asked.

In Ireland, he replied. He was afraid to look up into her face. She was a young teacher and he liked her very much. She had a lovely sadness and it was fine to sit in a room all day and look at her. Once she sighed sadly, and he sighed sadly, and she saw him and heard him. Then she looked into his eyes and smiled. She smiled at him alone, and when he left the room for recess, he went running through the school grounds with joy, tearing around because it was so fine, Miss Fargo seeing him, he himself, smiling at him.

She stood at the foot of the stairs a long minute,

not speaking; then he felt her hand in his hair. Thank you, John, she said.

He could never forget that; it seemed very strange, very fine.

It was the valley, the hot sun, and he was walking along a road, through the vineyard country, with Fat Garakian, Pete Tobin, and Rex Ford . . . going swimming, in the summer. Then it was the water, cool and clean to the body, and the diving, all the boys naked . . .

He could never forget them diving . . .

The war came along imperceptibly, and he was running through the town shouting. Peace, Peace, The War Is Over . . .

In his sleep the locomotive smashed through the earth, and he felt the longing for remote places, to go away from the valley, to cross the mountains, to reach the sea, alien cities, far places. And he saw vast ships . . . away . . . to all the places of the earth, to Tipperary . . .

He was riding in a train, crossing the mountains, alone, seventeen . . . then a motor bus . . . nineteen . . . then the subway in New York . . . twenty . . .

The snow, the multitudes alive . . . twenty-one . . . one day, one night, the earth, himself, over and over again, one day, one night, the earth again, and again himself, and again himself, again and again . . .

He was sitting in the small room, drinking . . . twenty-two . . . and the girl was sitting across the table from him, watching him. He had been silent a long time, ten minutes perhaps, drinking . . .

Then he said, What is it you asked?

She had been crying . . . one day, one night, to this, a new moment of talk, of being, and again himself, outside, in another's mind, with another meaning . . .

John, he heard her say, John, talk to me . . . what are you thinking? . . . John, is anything the matter? . . .

He saw himself standing before the house, crying . . . and he heard the girl talking to him, saying the same things over and over again . . . John, John, is anything the matter? . . .

But she had been telling him something . . . something amusing, something that brought back the image of the sea of his sleep, and the moments of being alive . . . this girl, he thought, it is too splendid . . . then he began to laugh quietly, looking into her face, laughing about it . . .

Tell me again what you said . . . she was a girl he had met at a cheap dance . . .

Tell me again, he said . . . I didn't quite understand.

She began to talk again, seeming frightened, smoking a cigarette, and all he could get out of it was two months on the way, and it was his, she was sure it was his . . . she had had other men before she had known him but after that she hadn't, would he believe her, she hadn't, she hadn't touched another man, over five months, she had been faithful . . . would he believe her? . . and now it was two months on the way and she was scared . . . she couldn't sleep . . . she just had to see him . . . what was he thinking?

You mean, he said, talking more to himself than to her, I myself, outside, in you, something growing, myself . . . is that what you mean?

Yes, yes, she said. John, please believe me . . . you will see, honest, you will see that it's yours . . . I've never loved anyone but you . . . I knew you didn't mean it to be this way . . . I didn't either . . . it just happened . . . but it's yours, honest, John, I'm not making this up . . .

He began to laugh again, feeling large . . . outside of himself . . . possessing all the earth. I, he said, I myself, something growing in you . . .

Then you will? she said. I could kill it . . . there are doctors and I could get it out . . . but I thought maybe you wanted to know . . .

He got up with anger and shook the girl, smiling at her after a moment. What are you talking about? he said . . . don't talk like a chippy . . .

You will? she said.

He began to laugh with all his might . . . it's mine, isn't it? he said. He sat down again, smiling at her, amazed. How does it feel in you? he asked. Do you mean to tell me you're sure . . . not one of those other things . . . do you mean to say it's pretty large?

Yes, she said, yes, large . . . I can feel it . . . we can rent a small place . . .

It is very funny, he said . . . Don't worry, sure, do you think I'm crazy? We'll move to a small house . . .

You want to have it? he said . . . you're sure?

Yes, she said . . . I want to see it . . . outside, living . . .

You mean, he said, to have it looking at things . . . standing up on earth, looking?

Yes, she said, I could go to a doctor . . .

Don't talk that way, he said . . . how is it making you feel? I'm beginning to feel fine, he said.

I feel fine too, she said; only I was scared . . . I thought you'd give me the money to go to a doctor . . .

Shut up, he said. If you say that again, I'll knock your teeth out . . .

But you love me . . . you love me, don't you, John?

Sure, he said, sure I love you . . . but that's not the point . . . tell me about it . . . do you sleep well?

I've been worrying, she said.

Stop worrying, he said . . . one day, one night, the earth, himself, then another, himself again, still another, and this other looking at the earth, through his eyes, seeing it, and a photograph, him holding the other, something small but of itself, and this girl . . . stop worrying, he said . . . we'll move to a small house and wait . . . I thought you were after money . . . I didn't quite understand what you were driving at . . . do you mean you want to see it, you yourself, outside, looking? . . let me feel where it is, he said . . .

He touched the girl, laughing with her . . . yes, he thought, I myself, outside, growing in her . . .

being the whole earth . . . you were talking so much, he said, I thought you were after money . . . I wasn't listening . . .

Sure, he said, sure . . . we'll move to a small house and wait . . . this is fine, he said . . . why didn't you say it plainly . . . why didn't you come right out with it . . . I thought you were after money . . .

He saw the earth growing in her through him, the universe falling into the boundaries of the form of man, the face, the eyes, solidity, motion, articulation, then awareness, then quiet talk, quiet communion, himself again, and yet another, to proceed through time, one day, one night, the earth, and the energy of man, and the face of man, himself . . . he began to laugh softly, touching the girl where it was growing, feeling fine.

Harry

This boy was a worldbeater. Everything he touched turned to money, and at the age of fourteen he had over six hundred dollars in the Valley Bank, money he had made by himself. He was born to sell things. At eight or nine he was ringing door bells and showing housewives beautiful colored pictures of Jesus Christ and other holy people—from the Novelty Manufacturing Company, Toledo, Ohio—fifteen cents each, four for a half dollar. "Lady," he was saying at that early age, "this is Jesus. Look. Isn't it a pretty picture? And only fifteen cents. This is Paul, I think. Maybe Moses. You know. From the Bible."

He had all the houses in the foreign district full

of these pictures, and many of the houses still have them, so you can see that he exerted a pretty good influence, after all.

After a while he went around getting subscriptions for *True Stories Magazine*. He would stand on a front porch and open a copy of the magazine, showing pictures. "Here is a lady," he would say, "who married a man thirty years older than her, and then fell in love with the man's sixteen-year-old son. Lady, what would *you* have done in such a fix? Read what this lady did. All true stories, fifteen of them every month. Romance, mystery, passion, violent lust, everything from A to Z. Also editorials on dreams. They explain what your dreams mean, if you are going on a voyage, if money is coming to you, who you are going to marry, all true meanings, scientific. Also beauty secrets, how to look young all the time."

In less than two months he had over sixty married women reading the magazine. Maybe he wasn't responsible, but after a while a lot of unconventional things began to happen. One or two wives had secret love affairs with other men and were found out by their husbands, who beat them or kicked them out of their houses, and a half dozen women began to send away for eye-lash beautifiers, bath salts, cold creams and things of that sort. The whole foreign neighborhood was getting to be slightly immoral. All the ladies began to rouge their lips and powder their faces and wear silk stockings and tight sweaters.

When he was a little older, Harry began to buy used cars, Fords, Maxwells, Saxons, Chevrolets and other small cars. He used to buy them a half dozen at a time in order to get them cheap, fifteen or twenty dollars each. He would have them slightly repaired, he would paint them red or blue or some other bright color, and he would sell them to high school boys for three and four times as much as he had paid for them. He filled the town with red and blue and green used automobiles, and the whole countryside was full of them, high school boys taking their girls to the country at night and on Sunday afternoons, and anybody knows what that means. In a way, it was a pretty good thing for the boys, only a lot of them had to get married a long time before they had found jobs for themselves, and a number of other things happened, only worse. Two or three girls had babies and didn't know who the other parent was, because two or three fellows with used cars had been involved. In a haphazard way, though, a lot of girls got husbands for themselves.

Harry himself was too busy to fool around with girls. All he wanted was to keep on making money. By the time he was seventeen he had earned a small fortune, and he looked to be one of the best-dressed young men in town. He got his suits wholesale because he wouldn't think of letting anyone make a profit on him. It was his business to make the profits. If a suit was marked twenty-seven fifty, Harry would offer the merchant twelve dollars.

"Don't tell *me*," he would say. "I know what these rags cost. At twelve dollars you will be making a clean profit of two dollars and fifty cents, and that's enough for anybody. You can take it or leave it."

He generally got the suit for fifteen dollars, alterations included. He would argue an hour about the alterations. If the coat was a perfect fit and the merchant told him so, Harry would think he was being taken for a sucker, so he would insist that the sleeves were too long or that the shoulders were too loose. The only reason merchants tolerated him at all was that he had the reputation of being well-dressed, and to sell him a suit was to get a lot of good free advertising. It would bring a lot of other young fellows to the store, fellows who would buy suits at regular prices.

Otherwise, Harry was a nuisance. Not only that, the moment he made a purchase he would begin to talk about reciprocity, how it was the basis of American business, and he would begin to sell the merchant earthquake insurance or a brand new Studebaker. And most of the time he would succeed. All sorts of business people bought earthquake insurance just to stop Harry talking. He chiseled and he took for granted chiseling in others, so he always quoted chisel-proof prices, and then came down to the regular prices. It made his customers feel good. It pleased them to think that they had put one over on Harry, but he always had a quiet laugh to himself.

One year the whole San Joaquin valley was nearly ruined by a severe frost that all but wiped out a great crop of grapes and oranges. Harry got into his Studebaker and drove into the country. Frost-bitten oranges were absolutely worthless because the Board of Health wouldn't allow them to be marketed, but Harry had an idea. He went out to the orange groves, and looked at the trees loaded with fruit that was now worthless. He talked to the farmers and told them how sorry he was.

Then he said:

"But maybe I can help you out a little. I can use your frost-bitten oranges . . . for hog and cattle feed. Hogs don't care if an orange is frost-bitten, and the juice is good for them the same way it's good for people . . . vitamines. You don't have to do anything. I'll have the oranges picked and hauled away, and I'll give you a check for twenty-five dollars, spot cash."

That year he sent over twenty truck loads of frost-bitten oranges to Los Angeles for the orange-juice stands, and he cleaned up another small fortune.

Everyone said he could turn anything into money. He could figure a way of making money out of anything. When the rest of the world was down in the mouth, Harry was on his toes, working on the Los Angeles angle of disposing of bad oranges.

He never bothered about having an office. The whole town was his office, and whenever he wanted to sit down, he would go up to the eighth floor of Cory Building and sit in M. Peters' office, and chew the rag with the attorney. He would talk along casually, but all the time he would be finding out about contracts, and how to make people come through with money, and how to attach property, and so on. A lot of people were in debt to him, and he meant to get his money.

He had sold electric refrigerators, vacuum cleaners, radios, and a lot of other modern things to people who couldn't afford to buy them, and he had sold these things simply by talking about them, and by showing catalogue pictures of them. The customer had to pay freight and everything else. All Harry did was talk and sell. If a man couldn't pay cash for a radio, Harry would get five dollars down and a note for the balance, and if the man couldn't make his payments, Harry would attach the man's home, or his vineyard, or his automobile, or his horse, or anything else the man owned. And the amazing thing was that no one ever criticised him for his business methods. He was very smooth about attaching a man's property, and he would calmly explain that it was the usual procedure, according to law. What was right was right.

No one could figure out what Harry wanted with so much money. He already had money in the bank, a big car, and he wasn't interested in girls; so what was he saving up all the money for? A few of his customers sometimes asked him, and Harry would look confused a moment, as if he himself didn't know, and then he would come out and say:

"I want to get hold of a half million dollars so I can retire."

It was pretty funny, Harry thinking of retiring at eighteen. He had left high school in his first year because he hadn't liked the idea of sitting in a class room listening to a lot of nonsense about starting from the bottom and working up, and so on, and ever since he had been on the go, figuring out ways to make money.

Sometimes people would ask him what he intended to do after he retired, and Harry would look puzzled again, and finally he would say, "Oh, I guess I'll take a trip around the world."

"Well, if he does," everyone thought, "he'll sell something everywhere he goes. He'll sell stuff on the trains and on the boats and in the foreign cities. He won't waste a minute looking around. He'll open a catalogue and sell them foreigners everything you can think of."

But things happen in a funny way, and you can never tell about people, even about people like Harry. Anybody is liable to get sick. Death and sickness play no favorites; they come to all men. Presidents and kings and movie stars, they all die, they all get sick.

Even Harry got sick. Not mildly, not merely something casual like the flu that you can get over in a week, and be as good as new again. Harry got T. B. and he got it in a bad way, poor kid.

Well, the sickness got Harry, and all that money of his in the Valley Bank didn't help him a lot. Of course he did try to rest for a while, but that was out of the question. Lying in bed, Harry would try to sell life insurance to his best friends. Harry's cousin, Simon Gregory, told me about this. He said it wasn't that Harry really wanted more money; it was simply that he couldn't open his mouth unless it was to make a sales talk. He couldn't carry on an ordinary conversation because he didn't know the first thing about anything that didn't have something to do with insurance, or automobiles, or real estate. If somebody tried to talk politics or maybe religion, Harry would look irritated, and he would start to make a sales talk. He even asked Simon Gregory how old he was, and when Simon said that he was twenty-two, Harry got all excited.

"Listen, Simon," he said, "you are my cousin, and I want to do you a favor. You haven't a day to lose if you intend to be financially independent when you are sixty-five. I have just the policy you need. Surely you can afford to pay six dollars and twenty-seven cents a month for the next forty-three years. You won't be able to go to many shows; but what is more important, to see a few foolish moving pictures, or to be independent when you are sixty-five?"

It almost made Simon bawl to hear Harry talking that way, sick as he was.

The doctor told Harry's folks that Harry ought to go down to Arizona for a year or two, that it was his only hope, but when they talked the matter over with Harry, he got sore and said the doctor was trying to get him to spend his money. He said he was all right, just a cold in the chest, and he told his folks to ask the doctor to stay away. "Get some other doctor," he said. "Why should I go down to Arizona?"

Every now and then we would see Harry in town, talking rapidly to someone, trying to sell something, but it would be for only a day or two, and then he would have to go back to bed. He kept this up for about two years, and you ought to see the change that came over that poor boy. It was really enough to make you feel rotten. To look at him you would think he was the loneliest person on earth, but the thing that hurt most was the realization that if you tried to talk to him, or tried to be friendly toward him, he would turn around and try to sell you life insurance. That's what burned a man up. There he was dying on his feet, and still wanting to sell healthy people life insurance. It was too sad not to be funny.

Well, one day (this was years ago) I saw Simon Gregory in town, and he looked sick. I asked him what the trouble was, and he said Harry had died and that he had been at the bedside at the time, and now he was feeling rotten. The things Harry talked about, dying. It was terrible. Insurance, straight to the end, financial independence at sixty-five.

Harry's photograph was in *The Evening Herald,* and there was a big story about his life, how smart Harry had been, how ambitious, and all that sort of thing. That's what it came to, but somehow there was something about that crazy jackass that none of us can forget.

He was different, there is no getting away from it. Nowadays he is almost a legend with us, and there are a lot of children in this town who were born after Harry died, and yet they know as much about him as we do, and maybe a little more. You would think he had been some great historical personage, somebody to talk to children about in order to make them ambitious or something. Of course most of the stories about him are comical, but just the same they make him out to be a really great person. Hardly anyone remembers the name of our last mayor, and there haven't been any great men from our town, but all the kids around here know about Harry. It's pretty remarkable when you bear in mind that he died before he was twenty-three.

Whenever somebody fails to accomplish some unusual undertaking in our town, people say to one another, "Harry would have done it." And everybody laughs, remembering him, the way he rushed about town, waking people up, making deals. A couple of months ago, for example, there was a tight-wire walker on the stage of the Hippodrome Theatre, and he tried to turn a somersault in the air and land on the tight-wire, but he couldn't do it. He would touch the wire with his feet, lose his balance, and leap to the stage. Then he would try it over again, from the beginning, music and all, the drum rolling to make you feel how dangerous it was. This acrobat tried to do the trick three times and failed, and while he was losing his balance the fourth time, some young fellow away back in the gallery hollered out as loud as he could, "Get Harry. Harry is the man for the emergency." Then everybody in the theatre busted out laughing. The poor acrobat was stunned by the laughter, and he began to swear at the audience in Spanish. He didn't know about our town's private joke.

All this will give you an idea what sort of a name Harry made for himself, but the funniest stories about him are the ones that have to do with Harry in heaven, or in hell, selling earthquake insurance, and automobiles, and buying clothes cheap. He was a worldbeater. He was different. Everybody likes to laugh about him, but all the same this whole town misses him, and there isn't a man who knew him

HARRY

who doesn't wish that he was still among us, tearing around town, talking big business, making things pop, a real American go-getter.

Laughter

"You want me to laugh?"

He felt lonely and ill in the empty class-room, all the boys going home, Dan Seed, James Misippo, Dick Corcoran, all of them walking along the Southern Pacific tracks, laughing and playing, and this insane idea of Miss Wissig's, making him sick.

"Yes."

The severe lips, the trembling, the eyes, such pathetic melancholy.

"But I do not want to laugh."

It was strange. The whole world, the turn of things, the way they came about.

"Laugh."

The increasing tenseness, electrical, her stiffness, the nervous movements of her body and her arms, the cold she made, and the illness in his blood.

"But why?"

Why? Everything tied up, everything graceless and ugly, the caught mind, something in a trap, no sense, no meaning.

"As a punishment. You laughed in class, now as a punishment you must laugh for an hour, all alone, by yourself. Hurry, you have already wasted four minutes."

It was disgusting; it wasn't funny at all, being kept after school, being asked to laugh. There was no sense in the idea. What should he laugh about? A fellow couldn't just laugh. There had to be something of that kind, something amusing or pompous, something comical. This was so strange, because of her manner, the way she looked at him, the subtlety; it was frightening. What did she want of him? And the smell of school, the oil in the floor, chalk dust, the smell of the idea, children gone; loneliness, the sadness.

"I am sorry I laughed."

The flower bending, ashamed. He felt sorry, he was not merely bluffing; he *was* sorry, not for himself but for her. She was a young girl, a substitute teacher, and there was that sadness in her, so far away and so hard to understand; it came with her each morning and he had laughed at it, it was comical, something she said, the way she said it, the way she stared at everyone, the way she moved. He hadn't felt like laughing at all, but all of a sudden he had laughed and she had looked at him and he had looked into her face, and for a moment that vague communion, then the anger, the hatred, in her eyes. "You will stay in after school." He hadn't wanted to laugh, it simply happened, and he was sorry, he was ashamed, she ought to know, he was telling her. Jiminy crickets.

"You are wasting time. Begin laughing."

Her back was turned and she was erasing words from the blackboard: *Africa, Cairo, the pyramids, the sphinx, Nile;* and the figures 1865, 1914. But the tenseness, even with her back turned; it was still in the class-room, emphasized because of the emptiness, magnified, made precise, his mind and her mind, their grief, side by side, conflicting; why? He wanted to be friendly; the morning she had entered the classroom he had wanted to be friendly; he felt it immediately, her strangeness, the remoteness, so why had he laughed? Why did everything happen in a false way? Why should he be the one to hurt her, when really he had wanted to be her friend from the beginning?

"I don't want to laugh."

Defiance and at the same time weeping, shameful weeping in his voice. By what right should he be made to destroy in himself an innocent thing? He hadn't meant to be cruel; why shouldn't she be able to understand? He began to feel hatred for her stupidity, her dullness, the stubbornness of her will. I will not laugh, he thought; she can call Mr. Caswell and have me whipped; I will not laugh again. It was a mistake. I had meant to cry; something else, anyway; I hadn't meant it. I can stand a whipping, golly

Moses, it hurts, but not like this; I've felt that strap on my behind, I know the difference.

Well, let them whip him, what did he care? It stung and he could feel the sharp pain for days after, thinking about it, but let them go ahead and make him bend over, he wouldn't laugh.

He saw her sit at her desk and stare at him, and for crying out loud, she looked sick and startled, and the pity came up to his mouth again, the sickening pity for her, and why was he making so much trouble for a poor substitute teacher he really liked, not an old and ugly teacher, but a nice small girl who was frightened from the first?

"Please laugh."

And what humiliation, not commanding him, begging him now, begging him to laugh when he didn't want to laugh. What should a fellow do, honestly; what should a fellow do that would be right, by his own will, not accidentally, like the wrong things? And what did she mean? What pleasure could she get out of hearing him laugh? What a stupid world, the strange feelings of people, the secretiveness, each person hidden within himself, wanting something and always getting something else, wanting to give something and always giving something else. Well, he would. Now he would laugh, not for himself but for her. Even if it sickened him, he would laugh. He wanted to know the truth, how it was. She wasn't *making* him laugh, she was *asking* him, *begging* him to laugh. He didn't know how it was, but he wanted to know. He thought, Maybe I can think of a funny story, and he began to try to remember all the funny stories he had ever heard, but it was very strange, he couldn't remember a single one. And the other funny things, the way Annie Gran walked; gee, it wasn't funny any more; and Henry Mayo making fun of Hiawatha, saying the lines wrong; it wasn't funny either. It used to make him laugh until his face got red and he lost his breath, but now it was a dead and a pointless thing, *by the big sea waters, by the big sea waters, came the mighty,* but gee, it wasn't funny; he couldn't laugh about it, golly Moses. Well, he would just laugh, any old laugh, be an actor, ha, ha, ha. God, it was hard, the easiest thing in the world for him to do, and now he couldn't make a little giggle.

Somehow he began to laugh, feeling ashamed and disgusted. He was afraid to look into her eyes, so he looked up at the clock and tried to keep on laughing, and it was startling, to ask a boy to laugh for an hour, at nothing, to beg him to laugh without giving him a reason. But he would do it, maybe not an hour, but he would try, anyway; he would do something. The funniest thing was his voice, the falseness of his laughter, and after a while it got to be really funny, a comical thing, and it made him happy because it made him really laugh, and now he was laughing his real way, with all his breath, with all his blood, laughing at the falseness of his laughter, and the shame was going away because this laughter was not fake, and it was the truth, and the empty class-room was full of his laughter and everything seemed all right, everything was splendid, and two minutes had gone by.

And he began to think of really comical things

everywhere, the whole town, the people walking in the streets, trying to look important, but he knew, they couldn't fool him, he knew how important they were, and the way they talked, big business, and all of it pompous and fake, and it made him laugh, and he thought of the preacher at the Presbyterian church, the fake way he prayed, *O God, if it is your will,* and nobody believing in prayers, and the important people with big automobiles, Cadillacs and Packards, speeding up and down the country, as if they had some place to go, and the public band concerts, all that fake stuff, making him really laugh, and the big boys running after the big girls because of the heat, and the streetcars going up and down the city with never more than two passengers, that was funny, those big cars carrying an old lady and a man with a moustache, and he laughed until he lost his breath and his face got red, and suddenly all the shame was gone and he was laughing and looking at Miss Wissig, and then bang: jiminy Christmas, tears in her eyes. For God's sake, he hadn't been laughing at her. He had been laughing at all those fools, all those fool things they were doing day after day, all that falseness. It was disgusting. He was always wanting to do the right thing, and it was always turning out the other way. He wanted to know why, how it was with her, inside, the part that was secret, and he had laughed for her, not to please himself, and there she was, trembling, her eyes wet and tears coming out of them, and her face in agony, and he was still laughing because of all the anger and yearning and disappointment in his heart, and he was laughing at all the pathetic things in the world, the things good people cried about, the stray dogs in the streets, the tired horses being whipped, stumbling, the timid people being smashed inwardly by the fat and cruel people, fat inside, pompous, and the small birds, dead on the sidewalk, and the misunderstandings everywhere, the everlasting conflict, the cruelty, the things that made man a malignant thing, a vile growth, and the anger was changing his laughter and tears were coming into his eyes. The two of them in the empty class-room, naked together in their loneliness and bewilderment, brother and sister, both of them wanting the same cleanliness and decency of life, both of them wanting to share the truth of the other, and yet, somehow, both of them alien, remote and alone.

He heard the girl stifle a sob and then everything turned up-side-down, and he was crying, honest and truly crying, like a baby, as if something had really happened, and he hid his face in his arms, and his chest was heaving, and he was thinking he did not want to live; if this was the way it was, he wanted to be dead.

He did not know how long he cried, and suddenly he was aware that he was no longer crying or laughing, and that the room was very still. What a shameful thing. He was afraid to lift his head and look at the teacher. It was disgusting.

"Ben."

The voice calm, quiet, solemn; how could he ever look at her again?

"Ben."

He lifted his head. Her eyes were dry and her face seemed brighter and more beautiful than ever.

"Please dry your eyes. Have you a handkerchief?"

"Yes."

He wiped the moisture from his eyes, and blew his nose. What a sickness in the earth. How bleak everything was.

"How old are you, Ben?"

"Ten."

"What are you going to do? I mean—"

"I don't know."

"Your father?"

"He is a tailor."

"Do you like it here?"

"I guess so."

"You have brothers, sisters?"

"Three brothers, two sisters."

"Do you ever think of going away? Other cities?"

It was amazing, talking to him as if he were a grown person, getting into his secret.

"Yes."

"Where?"

"I don't know. New York, I guess. The old country, maybe."

"The old country?"

"Milan. My father's city."

"Oh."

He wanted to ask her about herself, where she had been, where she was going; he wanted to be grown up, but he was afraid. She went to the cloak-room and brought out her coat and hat and purse, and began to put on her coat.

"I will not be here tomorrow. Miss Shorb is well again. I am going away."

He felt very sad, but he could think of nothing to say. She tightened the belt of her coat and placed her hat on her head, smiling, golly Moses, what a world, first she made him laugh, then she made him cry, and now this. And it made him feel so lonely for her. Where was she going? Wouldn't he ever see her again?

"You may go now, Ben."

And there he was looking up at her and not wanting to go, there he was wanting to sit and look at her. He got up slowly and went to the cloak-room for his cap. He walked to the door, feeling ill with loneliness, and turned to look at her for the last time.

"Good-bye, Miss Wissig."

"Good-bye, Ben."

And then he was running lickety split across the school grounds, and the young substitute teacher was standing in the yard, following him with her eyes. He didn't know what to think, but he knew that he was feeling very sad and that he was afraid to turn around and see if she was looking at him. He thought, If I hurry, maybe I can catch up with Dan Seed and Dick Corcoran and the other boys, and maybe I'll be in time to see the freight train leaving town. Well, nobody would know, anyway. Nobody would ever know what had happened and how he had laughed and cried.

He ran all the way to the Southern Pacific tracks, and all the boys were gone, and the train was gone, and he sat down beneath the eucalyptus trees. The whole world, in a mess.

Then he began to cry again.

The Big Tree Coming

Thinking, in the mazda-lamp light, the clock ticking night of January and the silent radio bulging with forty-six jazz orchestras, crooners, waltzes, tangos, quiet delirium; ah, lovely cigarette, swift steed leaping no thought, swiftly over no space, the lovely taste of death coming, loveliness in death coming, all children must perish, sweeping high over it, all children must lose their faces, all children must walk with their small legs out of it, all children must go.

Thinking January night all faces all forms all thought must go, must go, and nothing is coming, only slowly and swiftly the death of the moment, and the death of of of the death of who is it that thinks?

and whence? in the night, the quiet of waltzes, the hush of noise? who is it? who? and whence? which avenue of the living? which by way of the dead? Tall sad eucalyptus trees in January wind some centuries hence symphonically in no sadness of weeping.

And the stare of the gaping phonograph the shadow against the blur of monotony in wall-paper precise walls for precise seclusion all men must walk to moments ending all men must twist from print to earth and eyes that see must see not and ears that hear must hear only the sea and the smashing of space in accordion silence and all hands must lie deeply in the dirt and rot and rot and the garments of all men must be taken from their bodies and placed on wax dummies in the stores of pawnbrokers etcetera and the night which is ending will never end and the man who sits wakeful amid crumbling will return as a ghost to see his trousers being offered special one dollar and twenty-five cents and the same with his hat.

It is a merry time in January when the eucalyptus trees of tomorrow weep thoughtlessly for the men who died (dying now) a couple of hundred years ago which was last moment, and that boy smoking a cigarette was the one, it was he who was there and it was in a house there that he sat studying the gaping phonograph and where is he now? as well as his coat?

For there is some grace in dying quietly amid some fragment of a life some fragment of another's death two thousand years before some fragment of another's death and there is some grace in standing in the mazdalight our noblest contribution to sleeplessness our offering to children dying standing in the mazdalight awake and awake and dying and alive and the grace is a form of immobility as of quiet death and it is of the dance and the dance is of stone hard rock and never of fluid never of waves in motion and the dance is of smash of mountain graceful sky beloved pointlessness.

They will be saying then as they are saying now by turning inward and turning outward with the eye of thought to before and to after and they will be saying then as now that it was here during a moment of cigarette and mazdasleeplessness that it was here that he stood awake suddenly and suddenly alive in death and well now there is no house here only a tree a large fat thick selfish ruthless strong eucalyptus swooning in the wind and holding birds and it was here that a moment ago we saw his face quietly there in the light mocking the death and humbling himself before it and wanting it and mocking it and it was here almost that we heard him breathing the rock into his lungs and out again as thought as something from time and man and as something from the moment of himself but now there is no house here only this tree and what is the truth? what is it that we can say is not a lie even if it is a Christian lie? is it anything? or is it always an untruth? though we know that it was here that he stood?

And the talk we hear after all these moments and the crumbling of more rock and the shifting of seas and continents this talk that we hear is now a talk of silence and the words come blurred and there is no meaning there is no meaning and all is faint and sickly save the strength of the big tree weeping for no thought of man but weeping where the house stood and the talk is so quiet and it is so gentle that no one can say if it was the boy who spoke it or if it was maybe after the years the tree moaning it and there is no fact that can be stood on its tail and pointed to and there is no truth and all that comes through the space and through the quiet is the soft undulation of the thought almost sounded by mortal breath and it is of the upper limbs of the big tree swaying and breathing life and remembering the death of the boy.

But there is no fact and the issue is blurred. Historians stand bewildered and the rock which is crumbling crumbles more and the fact is in and out of the rock and in and out of the water coming in waves special delivery from the moon special one dollar and twenty-five cents for your best trousers and a dime for your hat and your ties are worthless absolutely unmarketable being polka dot ties.

You might as well smoke another cigarette and look again at the small calendar to make sure to see the fact on paper in print that it is January and you might as well presume that it is yourself looking and you might touch the gaping phonograph worshipping its silence, for it will be morning again before the tree bends itself westward again.

It is this year and it is now and already the tree and the rock are saying with the others who have speech that perhaps but only perhaps it may have been here in this spot on this earth that the boy stood dwindling to the pavement to the asphalt and to the bowels of it the bowels of the city and the earth and so you might just as well rise and yawn and say to yourself gentlemen I presume the hour is at hand and in the name of this universe I accept the nomination and humbly take my position among the solid ones now feeding flowers in cemeteries from Tokyo westward to Tia Juana and in all other directions humbly accept and humbly make my bow and platform speech to wit as follows gentlemen I shall do everything in my power and everything in my blood and bone and bowels to feed myself to sunflowers because they are strong and they resemble so much the sun and it is for the perpetuation of them that I humbly go down to make room for small and large and inarticulate imitations of the great bringer of light and life and laughter and leering and lice and all the other large and small things that make the scene so exasperating and lovely and make the scene so very very lovely and gentlemen you have my word of honor it is for the flowers that I say good day, I am going, going, gone.

The clock ticks language not yet precise but nearly so and the night is January. It was here that the boy quietly handing his coat to the man from the store said quietly to the man from the store well sir it is not a new coat and I have worn it for years but it will keep some poor devil warm another winter and that is all I care about to keep some poor devil warm another winter for we have the tradition to preserve and there is talk of time going away from us and there is a rumor that a couple of centuries long past due are crowding us and a number of unborn children are wailing their eyes out wanting to get on their feet and make a scene such as something about one child male wishing another child female and in them a multitude of children wishing the same thing only more savagely. So you see that the coat must serve to keep some poor devil warm another winter. Or else it will be all over and I being gone shall be gone utterly and the other shall be gone with me and the rodents will laugh and man will scratch his dead head and think well now that was remarkable those rodents laughing that way as if the joke was on us alone as if because they breed faster they don't die faster and it is remarkable and it is at that.

So fare thee well. It was here. It was in this house and now only a big tree is here, fare thee well, a big tree is here, so fare thee well, everywhere, everyone, seeking and never finding, everywhere, so fare thee well, lost everywhere, fare thee well, it was here, and again it is here but the day the night come and go and ah kindly one you were never in this house, so fare thee well, fare well, you were never here, and now the day is ending death is coming kindly over the emptiness and so fare thee well, ah gentle God, seeking thee we find the emptiness of the night and so fare thee well, the tree, the big tree is sinking its roots deep in preparation for the explosion from the earth and from time to thee to thee gentle and kindly God, seeking thee we perish unweeping and unhurt but wanting and wanting, so fare thee well, forever fare thee well, it was here and it was only a moment ago that we saw the boy's face grinning to God, and now there is only this big quiet tree, weeping for no one, moaning for no thought, seeking no God but being of God, forever and forever, farewell.

Dear Greta Garbo

Dear Miss Garbo:
I hope you noticed me in the newsreel of the recent Detroit Riot in which my head was broken. I never worked for Ford but a friend of mine told me about the strike and as I had nothing to do that day I went over with him to the scene of the riot and we were standing around in small groups chewing the rag about this and that and there was a lot of radical talk, but I didn't pay any attention to it.

I didn't think anything was going to happen but when I saw the newsreel automobiles drive up, I figured, well, here's a chance for me to get into the movies like I always wanted to, so I stuck around waiting for my chance. I always knew I had the sort of face that would film well and look good on the screen and I was greatly pleased with my performance, although the little accident kept me in the hospital a week.

Just as soon as I got out, though, I went around to a little theatre in my neighborhood where I found out they were showing the newsreel in which I played a part, and I went into the theatre to see myself on the screen. It sure looked great, and if you noticed the newsreel carefully you couldn't have missed me because I am the young man in the blue-serge suit whose hat fell off when the running began. Remember? I turned around on purpose three or four times to have my face filmed and I guess you saw me smile. I wanted to see how my smile looked in the moving pictures and even if I do say so I think it looked pretty good.

My name is Felix Otria and I come from Italian people. I am a high school graduate and speak the language like a native as well as Italian. I look a little like Rudolph Valentino and Ronald Colman, and I sure would like to hear that Cecil B. De Mille or one of those other big shots noticed me and saw what good material I am for the movies.

The part of the riot that I missed because they knocked me out I saw in the newsreel and I mean to say it must have got to be a regular affair, what with the water hoses and the tear-gas bombs, and the rest of it. But I saw the newsreel eleven times in three days, and I can safely say no other man, civilian or police, stood out from the crowd the way I did, and

DEAR GRETA GARBO

I wonder if you will take this matter up with the company you work for and see if they won't send for me and give me a trial. I know I'll make good and I'll thank you to my dying day, Miss Garbo. I have a strong voice, and I can play the part of a lover very nicely, so I hope you will do me a little favor. Who knows, maybe some day in the near future I will be playing the hero in a picture with you.

Yours very truly,
Felix Otria.

The Man with the French Post Cards

He looked, if he liked, like a sinful version of Jesus Christ, and he looked like a man who had lived a holy life so long that it had driven him insane and he had suddenly decided to destroy the holiness very swiftly. He would say: It is all the same; I do not care; and it would be very difficult to understand what he could mean. Every now and then he would be clean and inwardly calm; his face would be closely shaven and his thick reddish moustache would begin to seem something biblical; he would smile sadly, looking over the form chart, saying the names of the various horses, *Miss Universe, St. Jensund, Merry Chatter,* and so on.

I think he was Russian, though it was none of my business and I never bothered to ask him a personal question. He was always broke and always in need of a cigarette and I generally had ready-made cigarettes or the makings. He would never ask another man for a cigarette, and as a matter of fact he never actually asked me for one. I merely handed him a package or a sack of makings, and in this way we became friends. He looked deeply sad, generally, like some of the pictures of Christ, and it would be when he had shaved himself. Then suddenly he would stop shaving himself and he would be this way, with a beard growing on his face, for a whole week, sometimes two.

His poverty distressed me and I hoped somehow to be able to help him. We went now and then to a cheap restaurant on Third Street below Howard where a full meal with a steak for entrée could be had for only twenty cents, pie included. And I played the horses he liked so that if they won I would be able to give him part of the money without offending him. They seldom won, though, and it nearly drove him mad, making him mutter in his own language, Russian or Slovenian, and walk up and down the back room at Number One Opera Alley where we made our bets.

He was fifty but youthful, rather tall, rather lithe, and in his way rather distinguished. He was greatly down, but somehow his manner implied that it was all accidental and a mistake and that actually he himself was a man to command respect and admiration. I knew when he hadn't had a bed in which to sleep, and if the horses ran badly, I would sneak out of the bookie joint and run across the street to a rummy parlor and get into a game. At cards I used to be a little luckier than with the horses, and if I won, I would hurry back and put a half dollar in his hand so that no one would see it, and he would say nothing and I would say nothing. It was rather strange that he knew it was not for gambling and the next day I could see that he had had a bed and had slept.

Every day for several months I saw him and we talked of the horses. I knew dozens of other men like him and it was all a secretive sort of friendship, no man knowing the name of another and no man asking the name of another. I thought of him as the tall Russian, and I let it go at that.

Things went from bad to worse. All the men at Number One Opera Alley had a long stretch of rotten luck and I had my share of it too. I remember the day I went to the bookie joint with my last half dollar and listened to the tall Russian discussing the horses he thought might win. I made a bet on a horse named *Dark Sea* and sat down with the Russian to wait, smoking Bull Durham. I played the horse to win and it ran second, losing by a nose, and I believe this is the only time in my life that I ever became really excited. It was almost as bad with me as it was with the Russian, and each of us jumped up and began walking up and down, swearing to ourselves, looking at one another and swearing. That horse, he said, think of it, running so nicely all the way and then losing by a nose. And he began to swear in Russian. After a while I calmed down and said maybe it would be different tomorrow, the old gag among the horse players. The bright day was always tomorrow. That night I stayed in the rummy joint across the street, hungry, until two in the morning. After two I walked through the city and returned at nine in the morning to Number One Opera Alley. I was the first man to arrive, and I was feeling very cold, needing a cup of coffee very badly.

At ten the Russian came down. I had planned to keep my condition unknown if possible, but I couldn't manage it apparently and I knew that the Russian understood how it was with me; he came through the swinging doors and just as he came through I was walking toward the doors just to be keeping in motion, to waken myself, and he saw me and made the most painful face I have ever seen, as if it was his fault, not mine, but his, as if my having spent a sleepless night was his sin, and as if I was hungry because of him.

He said nothing, however, and began to look at Mannie's to see how the races looked. He was aching to smoke a cigarette but I had no cigarettes and no makings, and I couldn't think of anything to do. He finally went away without saying a word and returned in a half hour, smoking a rolled cigarette. He handed me the sack and I rolled one and began to smoke. The smoke wakened me and killed my hunger for a moment. I suppose he went out and begged, a thing which must have been disgustingly painful for him to do, but which he believed he *had* to do, and I began to be very angry with myself.

All day we talked about the horses, each of us knowing that the other had no money, and when there were no more races we went away. I don't know where the Russian went, but I returned to the rummy parlor and sat down. Late at night a young fellow I had once helped a little saw me and he sat at the table with me, telling me he had had a little luck. Before he left he handed me half a package of cigarettes and a quarter, not speaking of the matter, and I was able to buy a good meal and to smoke. Sitting in the rummy parlor, in the very bright electric light, I was able with my eyes open to sort of sleep, or halfsleep, and at two in the morning I did not feel greatly tired.

I walked the streets again until nine in the morning when I returned to the bookie joint. The Russian was already there, waiting to see how it was with me. He hadn't slept either and a four day beard was on his face. He looked angry and miserable and disgusted with himself. I handed him the package of cigarettes and we smoked.

Around ten in the morning he went away without saying a word, and when he returned a half hour later I knew that something was troubling him. He wanted to get us out of the mess we were in and he had an idea, no doubt, but it was troubling him. I hoped he wasn't thinking of trying to steal, but I could tell that the idea, whatever it was, was not a pleasant one. At last he called me to him, and I knew for the first time since we had known each other that he was a man who had once been greatly respected, a man of dignity. I could tell this from the polite manner in which he requested my company alone, out of the bookie joint. We stepped into Opera Alley, and he removed an envelope from his inside coat pocket. On the envelope was a French stamp. He looked distressed, disgusted and ill.

I want to speak to you, he said with an accent. I do not know what to do, and this is the only thing I have. It is up to you. I will do my best, then maybe we can have a little money.

He said this without looking into my face, and I began to feel unclean. This is all I have, he said. These are dirty pictures, he said. Rotten dirty French pictures. If you want, I will try to sell them ten cents each. I have two dozen of them.

I was disgusted with myself and sorry for the tall Russian. We walked down Opera Alley to Mission Street. I could not think of anything to say. It was really amazing, and I wanted to say something that would show I wanted him above all things to preserve his dignity; I wanted him to do nothing he himself did not wish to do, anything he certainly would not even be thinking of doing except for the fact that he knew I was broke and hungry and homeless. We stood at the curb on Mission Street. I could not speak, but I must have looked miserable, and at last he said, Thank you, I am grateful to you. There was a garbage can near the corner, and I saw him turn from me smiling like Christ himself is sometimes pictured as smiling and he walked away. When he reached the garbage can, he lifted the lid and I saw him drop the envelope into the can. Then he began to walk swiftly, thinking to himself, I thought, Well, at least, I offered to try to help him, even this way, and now I am free, and I saw him hurrying away, moving among the ragged men, still himself, still not wholly disgraced.

Three Stories

I. GREENLAND

Monday or Tuesday morning each week the postman brings me the *Herald Tribune Books,* from New York, and it is about writing of all kinds, and all kinds of writers. Many are being printed, many more are not, and I would like to know of a single city block where there is not at least one writer, and if there is a small village of fifty people somewhere in which a writer does not live I would like to know of this village. I would like to go to such a village and try to find out why one of the fifty people is not trying to tell the story of man on earth. I would like to walk into the village some morning and go quietly down the main street and all around it, looking at the houses and studying the movements of the inhabitants, because fifty people are many people and the moments of their lives are many. I would like to know of such a village, but I am sure there isn't such a place, not even in Greenland, and if you think I am joking, all you have to do is go down to the public library and look up the literature of Greenland, and you will find that the country is full of poets and writers of prose, and very good ones too. It is Greenland, though, and this is what I am coming to. The poetry is Greenland, and the prose is Greenland. Our country, America, is large dimensionally, and we have many writers, mostly unprinted, and my own writing is San Francisco, and it is not all of San Francisco; it is the western part, from Carl Street to the Pacific Ocean. It is Greenland, and not some clever young man, and you can praise God that this is so; not cleverness but the place, not art exactly but inevitability, the only thing, Greenland.

I am of Frisco, the fog, the foghorns, the ocean, the hills, the sand dunes, the melancholy of the place, my beloved city, the place where I have moved across the earth, before daybreak and late at night, the city of my going and coming, and the place where I have my room and my books and my phonograph. Well, I love this city, and its ugliness is lovely to me. And the truth is that I am not at all a writer and it is the truth that I do not want to be a writer. I never try to say anything. I do not have to try. I say only what I cannot help saying, and I never use a dictionary, I never make things up. All the prose in the world is still outside of books and largely outside of language, and all I do is walk around in my city and keep my eyes open.

Each Monday or Tuesday I turn the pages of this paper that is brought to me from New York and I look at the pictures in the paper and now and then I read a few words here and there, the names of new books and the names of writers. I want to know what is being written by the men who are being printed, because when I know what is being printed I can understand what is not being printed, and I think the greatest prose of America is the prose that is secret, and everybody knows that for every book printed there are twenty or thirty or forty that are not printed: America, as it was Greenland, the same.

Myself, I am a very poor writer. It is because I have never read the works of great writers, or because I have never been to college, and it is because the place is more important to me than the person: it is more solid, and it does not talk, and printed writers talk very much, and it is largely nonsense. I would like to know this: Is there anything to talk about, as a writer? I know there is much to be silent about, as a writer. I know there is much to talk about, *not* as a writer, the weather especially, ah, lovely, lovely, the sun so lovely this morning, and so on, but of course in different words, meaning the same. And this is so: today is the fourth day of sunny loveliness, and it is the first day that I have stayed in my room. It has been too good and I have been too happy, and now I must stay in my room in spite of the clear and warm air. I must stay here and try to speak quietly of this city, and not as a writer.

What it amounts to is this: I would like to try to say what all the unprinted writers would be apt to try to say if they were here, if they had lived during these three days of fine weather. And I am certainly not trying to write a story. The story is here of course. It is impossible to omit the story. It is always present, even if you write about the manufacture of clocks or electric washing machines—always present. It is my city, San Francisco, and it is the sun, very bright, the place, and it is the air, very clear, and it is myself, alive, and it is the earth, Greenland, not cleverness, America, not talk. This is the first story, and if you do not like the style you can stop reading, because this is it, the whole thing, the place and the climate of the place, and what we think is less important than what we feel, and when the weather is this way we feel that we are alive, and this feeling is great prose and it is very important, being first the place and then ourselves, and it is everything, Greenland, America, my city, San Francisco, yourself and myself, breathing, knowing that we are alive, drinking water and wine, eating food, walking, seeing one another, and it is all the unnamed and unknown writers everywhere, and they are saying what I am saying: that all of us are alive and that we are breathing, so if the style is unpleasant to you you can read the evening newspaper instead, and to hell with you.

THREE STORIES

II. VLADIMIR

Vladimir Horowitz was here a number of days ago, and one evening at the San Francisco Opera House he played the piano, and rich ladies applauded, and it made conversation. They are still talking of Vladimir's hands, and much of the talk is nonsense, and apparently it is impossible to get away from talking nonsense.

Vladimir came to this city and on Tuesday evening, February 27, 1934, he played the piano, and all the fat and thin ladies of wealth applauded him, and he took his money and went away, to Los Angeles, I think, and the ladies are still talking of him, breathlessly, though of course unsexually, art being of the spirit and not of the flesh. Well, it is laughable, and I myself heard several of the ladies talking of Vladimir's hands, and the talk was not of the spirit, not by a long shot; but of course this is not the point, and everybody has heard rich ladies talking. It is pleasant in a way, and it may be just as well that the talk was not of the spirit, and even the rich are basically only alive, breathing. If they go to concerts in order to have something to talk about, something other than the climate, it is because they *are* rich and because it is considered, in the best circles, shameful to talk about the weather. And the ladies must talk about *something,* and they cannot go on talking about Russia forever. But the point is this: myself again. I must explain that nothing I ever say is purely autobiographical, and the fact is that I am always speaking and thinking of the place and of the time of the place, and that I myself am included in the thought because it is inevitable. It is not a question of pride, but a question of accuracy and truth. I do so objectively: myself, of this place, of this time.

The evening Vladimir played the piano for the rich ladies I sat alone in my room, listening to him. The concert began at 8:30 o'clock, and I was in my room an hour earlier. I have seen the outside of the San Francisco Opera House many times, and I once sneaked in and saw the inside, at night, so I could see the place, sitting in my room. Around eight o'clock I began to see the big automobiles coming up to the Opera House, and I began to see the rich ladies alighting from the automobiles, and every lady was dressed in the most stylish mode. After a while the automobiles began to arrive in great numbers and special police began to blow whistles, getting the situation under hand.

Vladimir walked onto the stage and the ladies began to applaud; he played and bowed and played and bowed and the ladies applauded; then he took his money and went on to Los Angeles, and I sat in my room, smiling about it. What I hope is this: that Vladimir got a lot of money: this is the important thing.

From where I was in the city I could not hear the concert well, and as a matter of fact I could not hear it at all: I could only imagine Vladimir playing. Well, finally, at eleven o'clock at night I decided to listen to a concert of my own, and I walked swiftly to the beach, by the ocean: the beach is the place where hot dogs are sold and where you can ride the chutes and other things, and there is a merry-go-round at the beach: I went to the merry-go-round and listened to its music: this is the second story and it is probably a little more difficult than the first, and the whole point is this: that Vladimir did not play the merry-go-round music and the music of the merry-go-round happened mechanically and it was very bad but very splendid, being the music little children hear when they ride the merry-go-round horses and goats and lions and camels and it was the music of remembrance, so very bad, and so difficult to talk about, and still, it was very splendid and I sat alone listening to the concert and at midnight the music stopped and I applauded loudly and I said *bravo,* the second story, Vladimir and myself and the rich ladies.

III. AN OLD WOMAN BREATHING

The third story I will not write, because it is not a story that can be written: this morning from my window I saw the old woman who is bent half way to the earth and she was out in the sunlight, walking and breathing, and she was in black as she always is, locomotor ataxia, scientifically, and she was walking through the sunlight and I knew it was a story I could not write, and I said, I will say only this: that the old woman was in the light this morning, she herself, still alive, breathing, the little old woman bent half way to the earth, breathing this place and this time, the place, not cleverness, Greenland and America, the moment of our breathing, our greatest literature, not writing, *being,* not talking. Vladimir himself, not conversation, and his playing, and the machine music of the merry-go-round, and no children there at midnight, only the ghosts of all children, and finally the latest moment, the moment of the walking and breathing of the old old woman in the sunlight, and myself at the window, myself finally, Vladimir and the rich ladies and the Opera House and the ocean and the writers here and there in the sun and the warmth of the sun and clear air and the old woman, myself writing great prose in the only language, the language of being, Greenland and America, the young Russian at the piano, the unturning merry-go-round, and forever the Pacific Ocean, my beloved city, San Francisco.

Love

A little before midnight the thick fog that had been falling over the city became rain, and, walking along Sixth Street, Max stepped out of the rain into a doorway, wiping the rain from his face with a handkerchief. We can get out of the rain here, he said to his friend Pat Ferraro. We can go upstairs and sit down until the rain stops.

O. K., said Pat, but no fooling around.

Max pressed the button, and promptly, a bit too promptly, the door swung open. Business must be rotten, Pat thought. At the top of the stairs they saw a plump, middle-aged colored maid. She was smiling, trying to seem pleased to see them.

Good evening, Pat said to her. How are you, anyway?

Good evening, boys, said the maid. Right up front. Take the front room.

They entered the small front room, closed the door, and sat down. The maid went down the hall to get the girls. The place was very quiet, and they could hear the maid going down the hall. There were three chairs in the room, and a low tea table with a colored tile surface and an ash tray on it. On two of the walls were amateur oils of nudes. The nudes looked unhappy, a bit lopsided. On the lower shelf of the tea table were three copies of a pulp paper magazine called *Love*. The room overlooked the street, but the blinds of the two windows were drawn. Looking out the window, Pat watched the rain falling to the street.

It's coming down pretty heavy now, he said. Good thing we got out of it.

He sat down again. Do you know these girls? he asked.

No, said Max. This is the first time I ever came to this place. All the small hotels along this street are like this. You can stop anywhere along this street when it rains. These hotels don't rent out rooms.

No fooling around, though, said Pat.

Sure, said Max. We'll just talk till the rain stops.

They heard the girls coming up the hall. The girls weren't talking, they weren't laughing, and somehow their coming sounded a bit sad to Pat. He lit a cigarette. I hope they don't make me feel sorry for them, he thought. I hope I don't go away from here worrying about them.

The door opened, and the girls entered, three of them, in the usual sort of clothes. At first it was their bodies that he noticed, but after a while this bored him and he began to look into their faces, watching their eyes and their lips, wanting to know how they felt.

Each of the girls uttered the usual invitation, to which neither Pat nor Max made any reply. Instead, they remained silent, smiling. Then the girls seemed to forget the business they were in, and stopped using trade language.

Raining, isn't it? said the smallest of the girls. She was about nineteen, and she looked about as frightened as anyone Pat had ever seen. He began immediately to want to destroy the fear in her, to give her the sort of support she could never get in such a place, to get himself inside of her, simply by being in her presence, extend his strength to her.

Yes, he replied simply. Come here. I want to talk to you.

He saw her amazement. Defensively, she made another trade remark, and sat on his knees. He did not touch her, but held her hand. It was cold and the nails were long and ugly, tinted red.

What's your name? he said. He knew she would not tell him her name, but he wanted to find out what name she had made up for herself, and he wanted to talk with her.

Martha, she replied. Come on, she said, let's go to a room and have a party.

Martha what? he said. You look Jewish.

Martha Blum, she replied. Come on, honey, let's go make whoopee.

Cut it, he said. How've you been?

All right, I guess.

Max entertained the other two girls. The largest, who was very large, actually fat, sat in his lap, and Max began to touch her. She liked it very much because she imagined that after a while Max would go with her to a room and it would make a good impression on the landlady.

My, said Max, what lovely features you have, and he fondled her breast. You'd make a great mother.

Come on, honey, said the fat girl, let's go get married, let's go be man and wife.

Sure, said the third girl, why don't you two go to a room and enjoy yourselves?

Apparently, Pat thought, business had been terribly bad, and it had gotten the girls down. Maybe they were going to lose their jobs. They looked worried. They sounded *very* worried. It was pathetic the way they were wanting to seem desirable.

My, said Max, what solid thighs you have.

He got up suddenly, lifting the fat girl with him, and went to the window. He became suddenly severe, ignoring the fat girl, and when he sat down again she was afraid to sit in his lap. She looked a bit dazed, a bit bewildered. Her big body, her thick lips, the sensuousness of her, and these fellows sitting around as if she was made of wood or something. Pat could see that she was deeply hurt, and when she began trying again to interest Max, Pat began to feel rotten.

This is wrong, he felt; this is lowdown and rotten,

a dirty trick. This will make these girls feel rotten for weeks. They'll never get over this.

He looked across the room at Max. Come on, he said. Let's scram.

Don't talk nonsense, said Max. It's raining outside. It's not every night these girls can be touched by a couple of handsome young fellows like us.

Each of the girls tried to laugh, but their laughter sounded fake and pathetic.

Besides, said Max, if you girls are busy, you can run along. You don't *have* to stay with us. We won't mind sitting here without you.

Now is that nice? said the third girl. She sat in his lap, and Max put his arms around her.

Do you know, he said, you're not at all bad. There's something about you.

Then he made a sour face, as if he was smelling something unclean.

The fat girl stood in a corner, looking miserable. She was amazed. For Christ's sake, she said suddenly, you fellows ain't bulls, are you?

Don't excite yourself, said Max. Take it easy. My name is Max Kamm. I fight in the ring. Maybe you've heard of me. My friend's name is Pat Ferraro. He doesn't do anything. He plays the ponies and he cheats at poker. And it's raining outside. We're here to be out of the rain. Now if you want to run along, run along. If you want to stay and be sociable, stay.

Oh, said the girls.

Are you staying? said Max.

None of the girls got up to go. They seemed a bit relieved, but disappointed.

Fine, said Max. Now what shall we talk about?

He began to laugh and talk with the girls, and Pat lit a cigarette for the small Jewish girl. She inhaled deeply, looking at him sadly, making him feel sorry for her. He could feel himself liking the girl a lot and wanting to mean something to her, not the way it happened in these dumps, but really liking her, the girl herself, not her body and the convenience of performing the act with her, not to lie with her a few minutes and then go away, but to know her, inwardly, to be a part of that in her which seemed so admirable to him. It was foolish, but he was afraid he even loved her, really cared for her because of the deep sadness she could not hide, a girl who had to please anybody who happened to come to the place, old men and monsters. He was a bit amazed at what was going on in him, but he knew that if he had ever really loved a girl, if he had ever really cared for one, this was the girl. He began to speak with her quietly, while Max shouted at the other two girls, laughing with them, slapping their rumps, the rain splashing against the windows, sometimes impulsively with a sudden rush, sometimes softly, like weeping.

How do you really feel? he said.

She exhaled smoke, looking into his serious face, wondering if she could take him seriously, or if he was only kidding, killing time.

Oh, she said, expressing no specific emotion, I feel fine.

No, said Pat. Don't talk like a whore to me. Don't be like one with me. I really want to know. Is it driving you nuts? You look as if you were about ready to jump in the river. Is it really that bad?

She looked into his eyes again, and he could see that she thought he was simply talking, killing time like Max, waiting for the rain to stop.

I want to know, he said.

It's not so bad, she replied.

But you want to get out of it, don't you?

She looked toward the other girls to see if they were listening. Don't talk so loud, she said. If they tell the old woman what I've been saying, I'll lose my job.

Well, lose it, he said. To hell with it.

It isn't so funny, she said, if you can't get another job and you have no place to sleep and nothing to eat.

How long you been here? he asked.

Nine nights now, said the girl.

This girl, he thought. I'll get her out of here. I'll get a job and rent a small apartment and make her eat and sleep decently, and exercise. I won't touch her. I'll just stay with her until she gets on her feet again. I've got enough money for a week, and the first thing in the morning I'll go around to the employment agencies and look for a job. I've got to do this. I'd be a bastard not to try to help this girl.

He went on talking quietly with her, thinking about having her away from this life that was driving her nuts. He could tell now that she would go with him, anywhere. He could tell that she wanted to go with him.

He heard the doorbell ring, and someone coming up the stairs. Then he heard the maid opening and closing the door of a room, talking with a man. The maid came to the room, looking at the girls.

Number Eight, Martha, she said, and the girl got up from his knees, moving automatically.

He was stunned, and he got up with her, wanting to tell the maid to get the hell away from them, and leave them alone. He loved this girl. He didn't want her to be putting herself naked in front of some dirty punk with a stinking body and a putrid mind, and he would knock hell out of any bastard who tried to touch her. He would kill any man who tried to lay his dirty hands on her and drive her nuts, destroying the decency that was in her, that he alone could see in spite of the paint and in spite of the way she tried to talk, trying to be like a whore. He would break the whole God damn hotel to pieces and take this girl away with him, the bastards, making her want to die, scaring hell out of her.

He stood in front of the girl, staring at the maid.

Who wants to see her? he asked.

She's got to go, said the maid. There's a man out there who wants her. He was here last night.

Take me to the bastard, he said quietly. I'll kill him.

Max pushed aside the girl in his lap and grabbed Pat by the shoulders.

What the hell you talking about? he said, laughing. Let the girl go. What the hell's come over you, anyway? I never did see you talk this way before, and I *know* you're not drunk.

I'll kick hell out of anyone who tries to lay hands on her, he said. Nobody's going to touch this girl.

Jesus, said Max. You're nuts. He began to laugh at his friend. This *is* funny, he said. This *is* a gag.

Well, said the maid, if you want to go to a room with Martha first, you can go. I'll ask the other man to wait a little.

I don't want to go to a room with anybody, he said, and I don't want anybody to fool with this girl again.

Don't talk like an idiot, said Max.

I'll go get the landlady, said the maid.

Then he saw the girl, looking at him pathetically, run through the open door and down the hall. The maid left the room, closing the door, and he sat down.

Max was still laughing at him. For a minute, said Max, I thought you were serious.

The girls could think of nothing to say. Pat lit a cigarette. Well, he thought, that was funny, me acting that way over one of these girls. He began to laugh, inhaling and exhaling smoke. He went to the window and saw that the rain had stopped.

Let's scram, he said. Here, he said to the girls, buy yourselves a couple of drinks; and he handed each of the girls a silver dollar. Give them something, he said to Max.

Sure, said Max. Here's something for your girl. He placed a dollar on the table, and they left the room.

Walking down the hall, Pat saw room Number Eight, and he could feel the girl in the room, holding her job. He hurried down the stairs, thinking of the girl, feeling that he had been a coward not to have done what he had wanted to do, not to have busted the joint to pieces and taken the girl away; and at the same time he felt a little amused with himself, wondering how it had happened.

For a minute, Max said, I thought you were serious. I was ready to hit you on the chin and drag you out.

It was nothing, Pat said. These joints always depress me.

But he knew that he was lying, that it *had* been something, that if ever he had loved a girl, if ever he had really wanted to mean something to another person, it was the little Jewish girl, in the room, lying naked beside the man he should have knocked hell out of.

War

Karl the Prussian is five, a splendid Teuton with a military manner of walking over the sidewalk in front of his house, and a natural discipline of speech that is both admirable and refreshing, as if the child understood the essential dignity of mortal articulation and could not bear to misuse the gift, opening his mouth only rarely and then only to utter a phrase of no more than three or four words, wholly to the point and amazingly pertinent. He lives in a house across the street and is the pride of his grandfather, an erect man of fifty with a good German moustache whose picture appeared in a newspaper several years ago in connection with a political campaign. This man began teaching Karl to walk as soon as the boy was able to stand on his legs, and he could be seen with the small blond boy in blue overalls, moving up and down a half block of sidewalk, holding the child's hands and showing him how to step forward precisely and a bit pompously, in the German royalist manner, knees stiff, each step resembling an arrested kick.

Every morning for several months the old man and the little boy practised walking, and it was a very pleasant routine to watch. Karl's progress was rapid but hardly hurried, and he seemed to understand the quiet sternness of his grandfather, and even from across the street it was easy to see that he believed in the importance of being able to walk in a dignified manner, and wished to learn to do it the way his grandfather was teaching him to do it. Fundamentally, the little boy and the old man were the same, the only difference being the inevitable difference of age and experience, and Karl showed no signs of wishing to rebel against the discipline imposed upon him by the old man.

After a while the little boy was walking up and down the stretch of sidewalk in front of his house, unassisted by the old man, who watched him quietly from the steps of his house, smoking a pipe and looking upon the boy with an expression of severity which was at the same time an expression of pride, and the little boy kicked himself forward very nicely. The walk was certainly old-fashioned and certainly a little undemocratic, but everyone in this neighborhood liked Karl and regarded him as a very fine little man. There was something about a small boy walking that way that was satisfying. True Teutons appreciate the importance of such relatively automatic functions as breathing, walking and talking, and they are able to bother about these simple actions in a manner that is both reasonable and dignified. To them, apparently, breathing and walking and talking are related closely to living in general, and the fuss they make about these actions isn't therefore the least ridiculous.

People living in the houses of this block have been breeding well during the past six or seven years, and the street has a fair population of children, all of them healthy and interesting, to me extremely interesting. Karl is only one of the group, and he is mentioned first because he is perhaps the only one who has been taught a conscious racial technique of living. The other children belong to a number of races, and while the basic traits of each race is apparent in each child, these traits have not been emphasized and strengthened as they have been emphasized and strengthened in Karl. In other words, each child is of his race naturally and instinctively, and it is likely that except for the instruction of his grandfather, Karl himself would now be more like the other children, more artless and unrepressed. He would not have the military manner of walking which is the chief difference between him and the other children, and the mannerism which sometimes gets on the nerves of Josef, the Slovenian boy who lives in the flat downstairs.

Josef is almost a year older than Karl, and he is a lively boy whose every action suggests inward laughter. He has the bright and impish face of his father who is by trade a baker, and he is the sort of boy who talks a lot, who is interested in everything and everyone around him, and who is always asking questions. He wants to know the names of people, and his favorite question is *where have you been?* He asks this question in a way that suggests he is hoping you have just returned from some very strange and wonderful place, not like anything he has ever seen, and perhaps not like any place on earth, and I myself have always been embarrassed because I have had to tell him that I have come from a place no more wonderful than town, which he himself has seen at least a half dozen times.

Karl hardly ever runs, while Josef hardly ever walks, and is almost always running or skipping or leaping, as if *going* from one place to another was a good deal more important to him than leaving one place and reaching another place, as if, I mean, the mere going was what pleased him, rather than any specific object in going. Josef plays, while Karl performs. The Slav is himself first and his race afterwards, while the Teuton is his race first and himself afterwards. I have been studying the children who live in this block for a number of years, and I hope no one will imagine that I am making up things about them in order to be able to write a little story, for I am not making up anything. The little episode of yesterday evening would be trivial and pointless if I had not watched the growth of these boys, and I only regret that I do not know more about Irving, the Jewish boy who cried so bitterly while Karl and Josef struck each other.

Irving came with his mother and father to this

block last November, not quite four months ago, but I did not begin to see much of him until a month later when he began to appear in the street. He is a melancholy-looking boy, about Josef's age, and of the sort described generally as introspective, seeming to feel safer within himself. I suppose his parents are having him educated musically, for he has the appearance of someone who ought to develop into a pretty fine violinist or pianist, the large serious head, the slight body, and a delicate nervous system.

One evening, on the way to the grocer's, I saw Irving sitting on the steps of his house, apparently dreaming the unspeakably beautiful dream of a child bewildered by the strangeness of being, and I hoped to speak to him quietly and try to find out, if possible, what was going on in his mind, but when he saw me coming toward him, he got up swiftly and scrambled up the steps and into the house, looking startled and very much afraid. I would give my phonograph to know what Irving had been dreaming that evening, for I believe it would somehow make explicable his weeping last night.

Karl is solid and very sure of his stance, extremely certain of himself because of the fact that discipline prohibits undue speculation regarding circumstances unrelated to himself, while Josef, on the other hand, though no less certain of himself, is a good deal less solid because of the fact that a lively curiosity about all things impels him to keep in motion, and to do things without thinking. The presence of Irving on this street is solid enough, but there is something about his presence that is both amusing and saddening, as if he himself cannot figure it out and as if, for all he knows, he were somewhere else. Irving is not at all certain of himself. He is neither disciplined nor undisciplined, he is simply melancholy. Eventually I suppose, he will come to have the fullest understanding of himself and his relation to all things, but at the moment he is much too bewildered to have any definite viewpoint on the matter.

Not long ago there were riots in Paris, and shortly afterwards a civil war developed in Austria. It is a well-known fact that Russia is preparing to defend herself against Japan, and everyone is aware of the fidgetiness which has come over all of Europe because of the nationalistic program of the present dictator of Germany.

I mention these facts because they have a bearing on the story I am telling. As Joyce would say, the earth haveth childers everywhere, and the little episode of last night is to me as significant as the larger episodes in Europe must be to the men who have grown up and become no longer children. At least, seemingly.

The day began yesterday with thick fog, followed by a brief shower. By three in the afternoon the sun was shining and the sky was clear except for a number of white clouds, the kind of clouds that indicate good weather, a clear moment, clean air, and so on. The weather changes this way in San Francisco. In the morning the weather is apt to be winter weather, and in the afternoon the winter weather is apt to change suddenly to spring weather, any season of the year.

WAR

Hardly anyone is aware of seasons out here. We have all seasons all the year round.

When I left my room in the morning, none of the children of this street was outdoors, but when I returned in the evening, I saw Josef and Irving standing together on my side of the street, in front of Irving's house, talking. Karl was across the street, in front of his house, walking in the military manner I have described, looking pompous in an amusing sort of way and seeming to be very proud of himself. Farther down the street were five little girls, playing a hopping game on the sidewalk: Josef's big sister, two Irish girls who were sisters, and two Italian girls who were sisters.

After rain the air clears up and it is very pleasant to be abroad, and these children were playing in the street, in the sunlight. It was a very fine moment to be alive and to have love for all others alive in one's time, and I mention this to show that the occasional ugliness of the human heart is not necessarily the consequence of some similar ugliness in nature. And we know that when the European countryside was loveliest this had no effect on the progress of the last war, and that the rate of killing remained just as high as it had been during the bad weather, and that the only thing that happened as a consequence of the lovely weather was some touching poetry by young soldiers who wanted to create, who wanted wives and homes, and who did not want to be killed.

Walking past Josef and Irving, I heard Josef say, speaking of Karl: Look at him. Look at the way he's walking. Why does he walk that way?

I had known for some time that Josef resented the pompous certainty of Karl's manner of walking, and therefore his remarks did not surprise me. Besides, I have already said that he was naturally curious about all things that came within the range of his consciousness, and that he was always asking questions. It seemed to me that his interest in Karl's way of walking was largely aesthetic, and I didn't seem to detect any malice in his speech. I did not hear Irving make a reply, and I came directly to my room. I had a letter to write and I went to work on it, and when it was finished I stood at the window of my room, studying the street. The small girls had disappeared, but Karl was still across the street, and Josef and Irving were still together. It was beginning to be dusk, and the street was very quiet.

I do not know how it happened, but when Josef and Irving began crossing the street, going to Karl, I saw a whole nation moving the line of its army to the borders of another nation, and the little boys seemed so very innocent and likable, and whole nations seemed so much like the little boys that I could not avoid laughing to myself. Oh, I thought, there will probably be another war before long, and the children will make a great fuss in the world, but it will probably be very much like what is going to happen now. For I was certain that Josef and Karl were going to express their hatred for each other, the hatred that was stupid and wasteful and the result of ignorance and immaturity, by striking one another, as whole nations, through stupid hatred, seek to dominate or destroy one another.

WAR

It happened across the street, two small boys striking each other, a third small boy crying about it, whole nations at war on the earth. I did not hear what Josef said to Karl, or what Karl said to Josef, and I am not sure just how the fight started, but I have an idea that it started a long while before the two boys began to strike each other, a year ago perhaps, perhaps a century ago. I saw Josef touch Karl, each of them fine little boys, and I saw Karl shove Josef, and I saw the little Jewish boy watching them, horrified and silent, almost stunned. When the little Teuton and the little Slav began to strike each other in earnest, the little Jew began to weep. It was lovely—not the striking, but the weeping of the little Jew. The whole affair lasted only a moment or two, but the implication was whole, and the most enduring and refreshing part of it is this weeping I heard. Why did he cry? He was not involved. He was only a witness, as I was a witness. Why did he cry?

I wish I knew more about the little Jewish boy. I can only imagine that he cried because the existence of hatred and ugliness in the heart of man is a truth, and this is as far as I can go with the theory.

Sleep in Unheavenly Peace

Fog over San Francisco and a sky that is mad with mist and the splashings of high electric lights: a sense of being out of time, a sense of despair mingled with mockery; wet pavements, the usual people walking. When it is like this, the night business picks up; there is a deep and vague desire in the heart of man for death, and the whores carry death to any man, giving him enough of it to get him over the bad weather and to keep him alive awhile. But it is lovely weather for the girls, and in all the small hotels all over the city prosperity is becoming a fact. After midnight prosperity becomes a dance, swift opening and closing of doors, running up and down hallways amid pleasant unprintable language concerning an ancient and instinctive act, old men and young boys, big business, and the girls being very matter of fact, going from one job to another with the grace and dignity of priests performing sacred works.

This sense of being out of time has driven thousands of people from their homes into moving-picture theatres where new universes appear before them, with emphasis on man and his major problem: a thing called, conveniently, love. The Sunday midnight shows do a thriving business, and the people go back to their homes, sick with the sickness of frustration; it is this that makes the city so interesting at night: the people emerging from the theatres, smoking cigarettes and looking desperate, wanting much, the precision, the glory, all the loveliness of life: wanting what is finest and getting nothing. It is saddening to see them, but there is mockery in the heart: one walks among them, laughing at oneself and at them, their midnight staring.

The restaurants do well, too: there is something about eating, about being able to eat, being able to pay for food, to sit at a table after midnight, to be awake at that hour with food before one: the fog and the electric lights and a night moment of grief: something about eating food that is sad and amusing: nothing else to do: we can eat and stay alive and go and come, etc. We are still alive, at a table. We are still walking in the city. It is this year and all of us are still in the picture, sick with the sickness of frustration, eating.

There are other places, other ways of being with

the despair. It is all business, the return of prosperity. The little beer joints with their two- and three-piece orchestras are taking in a lot of cash and sending home a lot of slightly intoxicated people. Everywhere they are playing and singing, *The Last Roundup, Alice In Wonderland,* and other sad songs. At the El Patio a lot of young and old men and women are dancing. But until you enter the skating rink you cannot appreciate how sad the city really is. You've got to see the boys and girls skating to feel how bad it is, how miserably ill everyone is with frustration. They move over the floor like swift insanity, giving futility an aspect of grace. The swiftness of their movement is purely sexual, and it is this that makes the severe expression of their faces so overwhelmingly amusing, the sadness that goes around with them in spite of the fact that they are on roller skates, going around and around on a hardwood floor. But you do not really laugh; it is merely a feeling you experience, a sadness for man that can only be articulated through laughter.

Things quiet down after one o'clock. The corner newsboys, some of them over fifty, speak sadly of the horses, and the small fortunes they would have made if they had played their own hunches instead of the suggestions of sincere but annoying friends. Monday's paper is about Cuba, and a murder somewhere. The real news isn't in Monday's paper. It won't be in Tuesday's paper. It will never be in any newspaper. It has been going on so long that no one is noticing it any more. It is not even a subject any more, being *the fact,* the essence of the whole business, and having been forgotten when it seemed too frightening to dwell upon: the maddening desire in the heart of man for precision or death, the possession of all loveliness or complete disintegration.

Only the girls are able to speak of the matter intelligently. They seem to understand how it is, and at two o'clock in the morning they seem to be the only decent people alive. The way they talk, the accuracy of the unprintable language they use, begins to seem noble and eloquent, and they themselves acquire a loveliness that is universal. Up and down the stairs of the small hotels, old men and boys. Money is involved, but that is simply because this is a capitalistic society, and because the medium of exchange, even in questions of love and lust, has conveniently assumed the materiality of coin and currency. It is impossible to understand the absolute failure of capitalism until one has studied the manner in which the girls carry love and death to clerks and bookkeepers.

At three in the morning you are apt to come upon strange specimens of life, men made frightening by capitalism. They appear to be monsters, and merely to be in their presence horrifies; yet they speak English, they were born of women, they have names, they belong to the family of man. It is possible to speak to them. The one with whom I spoke was thirty-five. He said his name was Jones. He said he walked at night and rested during the day, standing up. He said it was easy; he had been doing it for years. He was not a Communist. I asked, and he said he was not. He was more afraid of me than I of him.

SLEEP IN UNHEAVENLY PEACE

His name was not Jones; he could think of no other at the moment. My question startled him, and his mouth fell open, increasing the horror of his face, the dirty beard, the haunted eyes, the filth, and the very long lower teeth. I felt great love for him, even though he was ugly with the vilest ugliness of man, ghastly sexual ugliness: anger, amazement, and the desire to kill or rape, in his eyes.

Not any of the girls are trivial: this is a fact that must be recognized. It is impossible to be trivial, being so close to the secret of man. Work ends for the girls at three, no NRA codes or regulations. After three they go to bed. This time to sleep. They say they sleep soundly, in unheavenly peace in the stillness and hush of the time of man.

Fight Your Own War

I am sitting in this small room, two or three months from now or two or three years from now, writing a story about a number of human beings marching in a hunger parade and writing about what is going on in their minds, about all the remarkable things they are dreaming and imagining in connection with themselves and the universe, when I hear a knock at my door, a very emphatic knock.

I know it isn't opportunity because opportunity knocked at my door a number of years ago when I was out, looking for a job, so I imagine it must be my cousin Kirk Minor, the best writer I know who does not write and does not want to write. Or else, I imagine, it is that young man with the sad face and the ragged blue serge suit who works for the collection agency and comes to my room once a month to inform me politely and nervously that unless I cough up with those four dollars I still owe that employment agency that got me a job in 1927 the case will be taken to court and I will be disgraced, and maybe sent to the penitentiary.

This young man has been coming around to my room so often that I know him very well and in a roundabout way we have come to be friends, even though on the surface we may appear to be enemies. I never did bother to ask him his name but he has told me all about himself and I know he has a wife and a young daughter who is always ill and a source of great worry.

At first I used to dislike this young man and I used to wonder why he worked for such a company as a collection agency, but when he explained about his little sick daughter I began to understand that he *had* to earn money somehow and that he wasn't doing it because he liked to do it, but merely because it was absolutely, almost frantically, necessary. He used to come into my room, melancholy with worry, and he used to try to look at me severely, and then he would say: See here, Mr. Sturiza, my firm is becoming very tired of your evasions, and we must have a full settlement at once. And I used to say: Sit down. Have a cigarette. How is your daughter? Then the young collector used to sigh and sit down and light a cigarette. Duty is duty, he used to begin, and I've got to be severe with you. After all, you owe our client four dollars. All right, I used to say, *be* severe. I don't owe anybody a dime. I owe my cousin Kirk Minor a half dollar, but he hasn't taken the case to an agency. Then we used to talk for about a half hour or so, and the young collector used to tell me his troubles, how bad it was with him, and I used to tell him my troubles, how bad it was with me, wanting to write well and always putting down the wrong thing, and then having to go out and walk to the public library to try to find out again how Flaubert did it.

The knock destroys the continuity of my thought, and I go to the door and open it. If it is my cousin Kirk, I think, I will reprimand him; if it is the young man from the collection agency, I will be polite, and I will ask about his daughter.

It is neither, however; it is a small man of fifty with a dull face animated momentarily by some exciting thought, and in his left hand is a large brown envelope, stuffed, no doubt, with very important documents. The man is a stranger to me, therefore I am greatly interested in him, hoping to be able to learn enough about him to write a good short story.

Enrico Sturiza? he asks, only he shouts it, and I begin to understand that something has happened somewhere in the world, something momentous, historic.

Yes, sir, I reply quietly.

Enrico Sturiza, continues the small man in a manner that suggests that I am about to be sentenced to death for some petty and forgotten misdemeanor, I have the distinguished honor to inform you, on behalf of the International League for the Preservation of

Democracy and the Annihilation of Fascism, Bolshevism, Communism and Anarchism, that you are eligible for active duty in the front line, and that as soon as you are able to get your hat and coat I shall be pleased to escort you in the Packard downstairs to the regimental headquarters. There you will be furnished a brand new uniform, a small book of instructions written in language comprehensible even to seven-year-olds, a good gun and a place to sleep.

The small man has made this speech in a lively and impressive style, but I am not greatly impressed. I pause, light a cigarette and suggest that my guest enter my room and sit down. He enters my room, but declines the chair.

Is there a war? I ask politely.

Yes, of course, smiles the small man, implying that I must be a dunce not to know. War, he announces, was declared this morning at exactly a quarter past six.

That's no hour to be declaring war, I reply. Hardly anyone is awake at that hour. Who did the declaring?

This question disturbs the small man, and he blushes with confusion, making a face and attempting a cough.

The full and written declaration of war was printed in all the morning papers, he replies.

I don't read the papers, I reply. I sometimes glance at the *Christian Science Monitor,* but not often. I am a writer, and reading newspapers spoils my style. I cannot afford to do it. But the war interests me. Who wrote the declaration?

The small man does not like me, and he refuses even to attempt to answer my question.

Are you Enrico Sturiza? he asks again.

I am, I reply.

Very well then, come with me, says the small man.

I am sorry, I reply. I am writing a short story about hungry people marching in a parade, and I must finish the story today. I cannot come with you. After I finish the story, I must walk to the Pacific Ocean for exercise.

I demand, says the small man, that you come with me. In the name of the International League, I demand that you come with me.

Get the hell out of here, I reply quietly.

The small man begins to tremble with rage, and I begin to fear that he will have some sort of fit. He turns, however, in a military manner, shouts that I am a traitor, and departs.

I return to my typewriter and try to go on with the story I am writing, but it is not easy to do so. A war is a war, and everybody knows how viciously the last war got on the nerves of writers, bringing about all sorts of eccentric styles of writing, all sorts of mannerisms. News of the war upsets me, and I begin to mope, sitting idly in my chair, trying to think of something intelligent to think.

In not more than a half hour there is another knock at my door, and opening it I look upon the handsome figure of a young man in an officer's uniform. He is obviously a well-bred sort of chap, through the university, cheerful, and not altogether an idiot.

Enrico Sturiza? he asks.

Yes, I reply. Please come in.

My name, says the young officer offering me his hand, is Gerald Appleby.

I am very pleased to know your name, I reply. Will you be seated?

Young Mr. Appleby accepts my hospitality, produces a cigarette case, opens it; I accept one, we begin to smoke, and a conversation begins.

Mr. Covington, says Mr. Appleby, paid you a visit this morning, I am informed. His report suggests that you do not—shall I say?—do not particularly wish to be escorted by him to regimental headquarters. My commanding officer, General Egmont Pratt, has suggested that I call on you for the purpose of carrying on a conversation, with the view, we hope, of convincing you of the urgency of your participating in the present war before civilization itself is threatened.

Appleby is very interesting. He is interesting because I can see that nothing short of a war, and nothing short of a threatened civilization, could possibly lift him from the narrowness and emptiness of his life.

What makes you think civilization is being threatened? I ask him. Where did you get that idea?

Unless we crush the enemy, young Appleby replies, boyishly evading the question, civilization will be crushed, and crushed so badly that the earth will again enter a state of utter barbarism.

Which civilization are you referring to? I ask.

Our civilization, says Mr. Appleby.

I hadn't noticed, I reply. Besides, I am heartily in favor of a return to utter barbarism. I think it would be very good fun. I think even the most highly sophisticated people would enjoy being barbaric for a century or so.

Mr. Sturiza, says the young officer, as one young man to another, I ask you to cease being flippant, and to join your brothers in the battle against the destructive forces of man which are now threatening to overthrow all the noble and decent emotions of man.

Are you sure? I ask.

We must fight for the defense of democratic traditions, and if need be we must die in the battle.

Do you want to die? I ask *very* politely.

For liberty, yes, replies Mr. Appleby.

I'll tell you, then, I say, how Pascin did it. I think he did it gracefully. He got into a warm tub, gently slashed his wrists, and bled to death, painlessly and artfully. There are, of course, a number of other ways, equally artful. I would not care to recommend leaping from a skyscraper. It is a much too hurried and fidgety way, one of those modern trends in suicide. I myself do not wish to die. It is part of my plan as a writer of prose to try to live as long as possible. I hope even to outlive three or four wars. It is my plan to stay alive indefinitely.

I cannot understand you, says Mr. Appleby. You are a strong young man. You are not ill. You have the erect posture of a soldier, and yet you pretend to wish not to engage in this war, a war which will end all wars, a war of history, an opportunity to participate in perhaps the most extraordinary event ever to happen on the face of the earth. Our air forces are perfect. Our gas and chemical divisions are prepared to destroy the enemy in wholesale lots. Our tanks are the largest, the fastest and the deadliest. Our big guns are bigger than the big guns of the enemy. Our ships outnumber by three to one the ships of the enemy. Our espionage system is functioning perfectly and every secret of the enemy is known to us. Our submarines are ready to sink every ship of the enemy. And you sit here and pretend not to care to be involved in this, the noblest war of all time.

Precisely, I reply. I have no desire to destroy the enemy. I do not recognize an enemy. Who are you supposed to be fighting? Germany? France? Italy? Russia? Who? I am very fond of Germans and of the French and the Italian and the Russian. I wouldn't think of so much as hurting the feelings of a Russian. I am a great admirer of Dostoyevsky and Tolstoi and Turgenev and Chekhov and Andreyev and Gorky.

Mr. Appleby rises, deeply hurt. Very well then, he says. Unfortunately, we have not yet obtained the required authority to demand the participation of all able-bodied young men, but our propaganda department is working night and day and we mean to put over a general election and to *win* the election. It is only a question of time when all you indifferent and cowardly fellows will be in the front ranks where you belong. I assure you, Mr. Sturiza, you shall not be able to escape this war.

Maybe this fellow is right at that, I think.

Come in again sometime, I suggest, and we'll have a little conversation about art. It is an inexhaustible subject; the more you talk about it, the more there is to say and unsay.

I return again, a bit sadly this time, to the short story I am supposed to be writing, but it is no use; the war will not allow me to write. It is like a shadow over every thought and it renders futile every hope for the future. Rather than sit and mope, I go outdoors and begin to walk, moving in the direction of the public library. I notice people, and I notice that something has come over them. They are not the way they were yesterday. It is a very subtle change, and it is hard to explain, but I can tell that they are not the same. I wonder if I am the same. Certainly I am the same, I say, but at the same time I cannot believe in what I am saying. The people, like myself, seem to be the same, but they are not. I can perceive the difference that has come over them, but I cannot identify the difference that has come over me. I am doing my best to remain the same, but in spite of my efforts it is not working very well. Each moment finds me slightly but definitely changed.

The change in the people is hysteria; it is not yet at a high pitch, but it is beginning to grow. The change in myself, I begin to hope, is not the beginning of hysteria. I am quite calm. Only I cannot deny that I am beginning to be a little angry, and unconsciously I have a desire to knock down the next young man who asks me to participate in the war; I believe unconsciously that this is the proper thing for me to do, to knock down such a fool.

In the evening I return to my room and find my cousin Kirk Minor listening to the phonograph. The music is *Elegy,* by Massenet, sung by Caruso. My cousin is smoking a cigarette, looking very calm, listening to the greatest singer the world has ever known, and, according to my cousin, one of the greatest men the world has ever known.

What about the war? I ask my cousin.

What about it? he replies.

How do you feel about it?

No opinions at all, says my cousin.

You're not telling the truth, I say. How do you feel? You're seventeen: they'll be taking you before long. How do you feel about it?

I don't like crowds, says my cousin.

But they'll make you go.

No, he says. They won't make me go. I hate walking in line. I don't enjoy wars.

They don't care about that, I say. They are working on the government and they will force you to go.

No, says my cousin. I will refuse.

They will put you in jail, I tell him.

Let them, I won't care, says my cousin.

Don't you want to fight for the perpetuation of Democracy or something like that? I ask him.

No, says my cousin. I dislike walking in an army very much. It embarrasses me. I like to walk alone.

Well, I tell him, they sent two officers out here today, and I had to insult both of them.

That's fine, says my cousin. You didn't start the war. Let the men who started the war fight it. You're supposed to be a writer of stories, though I doubt it.

That's your opinion, I tell him. Get the hell out of here; I am going to start writing again.

A week later I am visited by a very stylishly dressed

young woman who talks glibly and smokes cigarettes nervously.

We are determined to have your cooperation, Mr. Sturiza, she says. We have learned that you are a writer of short stories, and we should like to have you as a member of our local propaganda department. Your work will be to write human interest stories about young men volunteering to save civilization, heroic sacrifices of mothers, wives, sisters and daughters, and so on. You will be well remunerated, and there will be many opportunities for advancement.

I'm sorry, I say, I'm no good at human interest stories.

You needn't worry about that, says the young lady. All the forms have been scientifically devised so that the maximum of emotional effect will be established in the feelings of the public, and you simply change the names, addresses and other minor details. It is very simple.

I can imagine, I say, but I don't want the job.

It pays fifty dollars a week, says the young woman, and you have the rank of first lieutenant. You participate in all military social functions, and let me tell you you will meet a lot of people who will be useful to you after the war.

Fifty dollars a week is more money than I ever hoped to earn, and people are very interesting to me.

I'm sorry, I say, the job doesn't interest me.

The young woman goes away, asking me to think the matter over. She is stopping at one of the best hotels in town, and wonders if I wouldn't care to visit her some evening for a drink and a chat. I myself wonder.

Two months later my cousin Kirk Minor comes into my room with a morning paper. In the paper is the information that all able-bodied men will be forced to participate in the war which has not been going any too well for the side which is supposed to be our side. Our casualties have been almost as great as the casualties of the enemy: approximately one million men, twice that number injured. There have been liberty loan drives, mass meetings and thick headlines for weeks.

I read the news and sit down to smoke another cigarette.

Well, I say, this means that they're going to get me after all.

What do you intend to do? my cousin asks.

I have decided, I say, not to allow myself to become involved.

Five days later I receive a letter ordering me to be at regimental headquarters the following morning at eight. The following morning at eight I am in my room, trying to write a short story. At eleven minutes past two in the afternoon Mr. Covington, the small man who visited me first, and four other men like him enter my room. In the hall are two military policemen, and downstairs are two large and expensive automobiles.

Enrico Sturiza? says Mr. Covington.

Yes, I reply.

As chairman of the Committee for the Study of Cases of Desertion in this district, which is the 47th district of San Francisco, it is my duty to question you in regard to your failure to appear for mobilization this morning. Did you receive official letter number 247-Z?

I suppose the letter I received was official letter number 247-Z, I reply.

Did you read it?

Yes, I read it.

Then why, if you please, did you not report this morning for mobilization?

Yes, says another of the small men, why?

Yes, why? says another.

Yes, why? says the third.

The fourth, I think, is incapable of speech. He says nothing.

I had a short story to write, I reply to the Committee, and I was engaged in writing it when I was honored by your visit.

I shall have to ask you, says Mr. Covington, to make direct replies. Were you so ill that you could not report for mobilization?

No, I reply, I was very well, and still am. I never felt better in my life.

Then, says Mr. Covington, I regret to inform you that you are now under arrest as a deserter.

I am standing over my typewriter and looking down on a bundle of clean yellow paper, and I am thinking to myself *this is my room and I have created a small civilization in this room, and this place is the universe to me, and I have no desire to be taken away from this place,* and suddenly I know that I have struck Mr. Covington and that he has fallen to the floor of my room, and that I am doing my best to strike the other members of the Committee, and they are holding my arms, the four members of the Committee and the two military police, and the only thing I can think is *why in hell don't you bastards fight your own war, you old fogies who destroyed millions of men in the last war, why don't you fight your own God damn wars,* but I cannot say anything, and one of the members of the Committee is telling me, *if Mr. Covington dies, we shall have to shoot you, Mr. Sturiza, it will be our painful duty to shoot you, Mr. Sturiza; if Mr. Covington does not die, you may get off with twenty years in the penitentiary, Mr. Sturiza, but if he dies, it will be our painful duty to shoot you;* and going down the stairs this small old man is saying this to me over and over again.

Common Prayer

The plains, Lord, and all the silences of mind, lost corridors, pillars, the places where we walked, the faces we saw, and the singing of little children. But most of all hieroglyphics, the holiness, the figure in stone, the simple line, our language, the articulated curve of, let us say, leaf and dream and smile, the fall of hand, touch of limbs, love of universes, no fear of death and some longing. Yea, and the light, our sun, Lord, and the sun of unknown men, the mornings lost in time of giants and pigmies everywhere, a man named Bach, a man named Cezanne, and the others with lost names, the multitudes now come together as one, nameless, our face, the mourning of anonymous mobs, our form, stature, men walking in the light, in several places, Asia to begin with, Europe, Africa, and across that sea of mind and fluid, Atlantic, westward to this place, America, and the marching of Marines, and the grinning of pale Wilson, freedom for Lithuania, hail Poland, and the counties of Texas, sweet melons and poverty, our thanks, Lord. And for numerals, so that a record of our grief may be made, one for sorrow, two for pain, three for madness, and a thousand and ten thousand and the reckoning of eternity, light years, the beard of Darwin, let us say, the eyes of Einstein, let us assume, the fingers of the great polish pianist, and let us assume all things numerically, the wealth of Ford, of Mellon, the poverty of—let us think of a worthy name—of Pound, shall we say, or shall we say, the unknown, the nameless young man of Clay County, Iowa, sitting alone, writing stories for God and the *Saturday Evening Post*—that is, the idea of the thing, the anonymity of the horror, the loneliness, waiting for fame and a brief note, you, the name, my lad, you are famous, a story in the *Post,* thank you, Lord.

The Shepherd's Daughter

It is the opinion of my grandmother, God bless her, that all men should labor, and at the table, a moment ago, she said to me: You must learn to do some good work, the making of some item useful to man, something out of clay, or out of wood, or metal, or cloth. It is not proper for a young man to be ignorant of an honorable craft. Is there anything you can make? Can you make a simple table, a chair, a plain dish, a rug, a coffee pot? Is there anything you can do?

And my grandmother looked at me with anger.

I know, she said, you are supposed to be a writer, and I suppose you are. You certainly smoke enough cigarettes to be anything, and the whole house is full of the smoke, but you must learn to make solid things, things that can be used, that can be seen and touched.

There was a king of the Persians, said my grandmother, and he had a son, and this boy fell in love with a shepherd's daughter. He went to his father and he said, My lord, I love a shepherd's daughter, and I would have her for my wife. And the king said, I am king and you are my son and when I die you shall be king, how can it be that you would marry the daughter of a shepherd? And the son said, My lord, I do not know but I know that I love this girl and would have her for my queen.

The king saw that his son's love for the girl was from God, and he said, I will send a message to her. And he called a messenger to him and he said, Go to the shepherd's daughter and say that my son loves her and would have her for his wife. And the messenger went to the girl and he said, The king's son loves you and would have you for his wife. And the girl said, What labor does he do? And the messenger said, Why, he is the son of the king; he does no labor. And the girl said, He must learn to do some labor. And the messenger returned to the king and spoke the words of the shepherd's daughter.

The king said to his son, The shepherd's daughter wishes you to learn some craft. Would you still have her for your wife? And the son said, Yes, I will learn to weave straw rugs. And the boy was taught to weave rugs of straw, in patterns and in colors and with ornamental designs, and at the end of three days he was making very fine straw rugs, and the messenger returned to the shepherd's daughter, and he said, These rugs of straw are the work of the king's son.

And the girl went with the messenger to the king's palace, and she became the wife of the king's son.

One day, said my grandmother, the king's son was walking through the streets of Bagdad, and he came upon an eating place which was so clean and cool that he entered it and sat at a table.

This place, said my grandmother, was a place of thieves and murderers, and they took the king's son and placed him in a large dungeon where many great men of the city were being held, and the thieves and murderers were killing the fattest of the men and feeding them to the leanest of them, and making sport of it. The king's son was of the leanest of the men, and it was not known that he was the son of the king of the Persians, so his life was spared, and he said to the thieves and murderers, I am a weaver of straw rugs and these rugs have great value. And they brought him straw and asked him to weave and in three days he weaved three rugs, and he said, Carry these rugs to the palace of the king of the Persians, and for each rug he will give you a hundred gold pieces of money. And the rugs were carried to the palace of the king, and when the king saw the rugs he saw that they were the work of his son and he took the rugs to the shepherd's daughter and he said, These rugs were brought to the palace and they are the work of my son who is lost. And the shepherd's daughter took each rug and looked at it closely and in the design of each rug she saw in the written language of the

Persians a message from her husband, and she related this message to the king.

And the king, said my grandmother, sent many soldiers to the place of the thieves and murderers, and the soldiers rescued all the captives and killed all the thieves and murderers, and the king's son was returned safely to the palace of his father, and to the company of his wife, the little shepherd's daughter. And when the boy went into the palace and saw again his wife, he humbled himself before her and he embraced her feet, and he said, My love, it is because of you that I am alive, and the king was greatly pleased with the shepherd's daughter.

Now, said my grandmother, do you see why every man should learn an honorable craft?

I see very clearly, I said, and as soon as I earn enough money to buy a saw and a hammer and a piece of lumber I shall do my best to make a simple chair or a shelf for books.

Li Po, Selected Poems

Clarice Lispector, The Hour of the Star
The Passion According to G. H.

Federico García Lorca, Selected Poems*
Three Tragedies

Nathaniel Mackey, Splay Anthem

Xavier de Maistre, Voyage Around My Room

Stéphane Mallarmé, Selected Poetry and Prose*

Javier Marías, Your Face Tomorrow (3 volumes)

Bernadette Mayer, The Bernadette Mayer Reader
Midwinter Day

Carson McCullers, The Member of the Wedding

Thomas Merton, New Seeds of Contemplation
The Way of Chuang Tzu

Henri Michaux, A Barbarian in Asia

Dunya Mikhail, The Beekeeper

Henry Miller, The Colossus of Maroussi
Big Sur & the Oranges of Hieronymus Bosch

Yukio Mishima, Confessions of a Mask
Death in Midsummer
Star

Eugenio Montale, Selected Poems*

Vladimir Nabokov, Laughter in the Dark
Nikolai Gogol
The Real Life of Sebastian Knight

Pablo Neruda, The Captain's Verses*
Love Poems*

Charles Olson, Selected Writings

Mary Oppen, Meaning a Life

George Oppen, New Collected Poems

Wilfred Owen, Collected Poems

Hiroko Oyamada, The Factory

Michael Palmer, The Laughter of the Sphinx

Nicanor Parra, Antipoems*

Boris Pasternak, Safe Conduct

Kenneth Patchen
Memoirs of a Shy Pornographer

Octavio Paz, Poems of Octavio Paz

Victor Pelevin, Omon Ra

Alejandra Pizarnik
Extracting the Stone of Madness

Ezra Pound, The Cantos
New Selected Poems and Translations

Raymond Queneau, Exercises in Style

Qian Zhongshu, Fortress Besieged

Raja Rao, Kanthapura

Herbert Read, The Green Child

Kenneth Rexroth, Selected Poems

Keith Ridgway, Hawthorn & Child

Rainer Maria Rilke
Poems from the Book of Hours

Arthur Rimbaud, Illuminations*
A Season in Hell and The Drunken Boat*

Evelio Rosero, The Armies

Fran Ross, Oreo

Joseph Roth, The Emperor's Tomb
The Hotel Years

Raymond Roussel, Locus Solus

Ihara Saikaku, The Life of an Amorous Woman

Nathalie Sarraute, Tropisms

Jean-Paul Sartre, Nausea

Delmore Schwartz
In Dreams Begin Responsibilities

Hasan Shah, The Dancing Girl

W. G. Sebald, The Emigrants
The Rings of Saturn

Anne Serre, The Governesses

Stevie Smith, Best Poems

Gary Snyder, Turtle Island

Dag Solstad, Professor Andersen's Night

Muriel Spark, The Driver's Seat
Loitering with Intent

Antonio Tabucchi, Pereira Maintains

Junichiro Tanizaki, The Maids

Yoko Tawada, The Emissary
Memoirs of a Polar Bear

Dylan Thomas, A Child's Christmas in Wales
Collected Poems

Uwe Timm, The Invention of Curried Sausage

Tomas Tranströmer, The Great Enigma

Leonid Tsypkin, Summer in Baden-Baden

Tu Fu, Selected Poems

Paul Valéry, Selected Writings

Enrique Vila-Matas, Bartleby & Co.

Elio Vittorini, Conversations in Sicily

Rosmarie Waldrop, Gap Gardening

Robert Walser, The Assistant
The Tanners
The Walk

Eliot Weinberger, An Elemental Thing
The Ghosts of Birds

Nathanael West, The Day of the Locust
Miss Lonelyhearts

Tennessee Williams, The Glass Menagerie
A Streetcar Named Desire

William Carlos Williams, Selected Poems
Spring and All

Louis Zukofsky, "A"

*BILINGUAL EDITION

For a complete listing, request a free catalog from New Directions, 80 8th Avenue, New York, NY 10011 or visit us online at **ndbooks.com**